Spinsters

Spinsters

pagan kennedy

HIGH RISK BOOKS

NEW YORK / LONDON

First published 1995 by
High Risk Books/Serpent's Tail
4 Blackstock Mews, London N4 2BT
and 180 Varick Street, 10th floor, New York, NY 10014

Reprinted 1995

Library of Congress Catalog Card Number: 95-67407

A full catalogue record for this book can be obtained from
the British Library on request

Cover design by Rex Ray
Set in 11pt Janson by CentraCet Limited, Cambridge
Printed in Finland by Werner Söderström Oy

Spinsters

Chapter One

THE STORY OF Doris and me began
when we stood before Dad's empty bed, and she said,
'What now?' I was for staying, of course. I didn't
want to miss any shift or tickle of sunlight that fell on
the dark floors of that house. Besides, I had long
looked forward to growing old with Doris there, the
two of us becoming hardly more than shifts of light
ourselves, our faces sinking into wrinkles until no one
could tell us apart. But she said it just plain didn't
make sense to stay—two ladies living in such a house.

And then one morning, she handed me a
letter and said, 'What do you think, Fran?' It was
from our Aunt Katherine, down in Virginia. The
letter lamented our father's death, then ended asking
if we might like to live with her. 'Girls,' it said in the
careful script of a woman who has plenty of time,
'you were always my favorites. Come and keep this
old woman company.' I held the paper close to my

face and sniffed at it, as if its smell had some bearing on my decision. It smelled of spinster, the sweet musty fragrance of an etiquette book.

I am not a believer in fate, but as I read through that letter, the design of my life became clear. Doris and I—in our thirties—were still too young to be old maids. It seemed to me then that we were meant to live with Aunt Katherine, under whose stern eye we would be spinsters-in-training.

We had last been to her house when both our parents were still alive; I remembered it as filled with strange glass paperweights, dolls that belonged to a girl who had died of whooping cough, a grandfather clock that incorrectly displayed the phases of the moon. It was near the seashore, and by day all of us—Mom, Dad, Doris and I—sat on the sand in the sun, thinking of nothing, talking in half-sentences, in a daze that I later realized was perfect happiness.

'Yes,' I said, putting the letter back in the envelope, 'that's where we must go.'

THEN CAME THE awful packing, when everything had to be put in the basement before the renters came. We cleaned out Dad's drawers, sifting through coins, cuff links, shirt stays, pills. I volunteered to take his clothes to the Goodwill just so I could be alone in the car with his aroma of medicine and cedar. Can I be blamed if I buried my face in one of his shirts before I got out of the car? The smell brought him back to me as he had been years ago, when in the middle of the night I'd found him in the dark, by an open window in the kitchen. The crickets were as loud and regular as the creaking of a rocking chair.

He had his elbows on the sill and was leaning so far out of the window that it seemed he was about climb through it and sneak away from us.

I said, 'Anything wrong, Dad?' He carefully backed out of the window and stood up. When he turned toward me, I barely recognized him. There was a look of confusion on his handsome old face. 'I'm doing what I always told you girls you shouldn't do,' he said. 'Thinking about what I wish had happened differently, instead of counting my blessings.'

'What would you have wanted different?' I asked, though I knew—of course I knew. One look at him was enough, the way his clothes hung too big on him, as if they were someone else's. Still, there's always more you don't know, even about the ones you love, and I felt that night I wasn't talking to my father but to the person he always kept hidden from us, the one who maybe felt bitter about the way things had turned out.

'Oh . . . ,' he began, turning to look out the window again. Then he shifted something about himself and became again the father I knew, the one who regretted nothing. 'I'll tell you my blessings,' he said. 'Two sweet, doting daughters.'

I used to torture myself by remembering things like that—thinking how a man who was filled only with light and love can die so terribly. That's why, when I parked in front of the Goodwill, I wished I could've lied to Doris and kept Dad's clothes. After all he'd suffered, I couldn't bear to have some stranger wearing the shirts he'd been so proud of. Even when he could barely sit up, he still wore his collars starched.

Somehow I managed to gather his clothes in my arms though, and bring them in and lay them on the counter. A woman rifled through Dad's things, handed me a stub of paper, then dropped them onto a heap. Seeing his clothes fall on that pile of anonymous sleeves and pant legs and scarves—that was the moment it dawned on me how gone from us he really was.

WE DECIDED TO drive the Valiant to Aunt Katherine's so we'd have the car down there, even though I feared flat tires and dirty motels on the way. The first day, we pulled over at a rest stop that was recommended in our *Esso Guide to the American Highway*. Doris stepped gingerly over the brittle grass to get a view of the river. Funny, but even she looked the proper spinster then—a dress-suit with a hanky tucked up her sleeve. I remember, too, that her hair had just been done, the curls stiff as meringue. I went into the visitors' center, where a park ranger stood behind rows of pamphlets and maps. 'Welcome to Delaware, Ma'am,' he said. I borrowed a newspaper from him, bought a bottle of Coke, and went outside to sit on a picnic bench.

It was the year of extraordinary and terrible news. That day, as I remember, the paper was full of the business at Columbia University. The sun falling through the fir trees dappled the picture of students yelling and gesturing, and below—in his own story—handsome Bobby Kennedy, our father's favorite, shaking hands with someone.

When I brought the paper back inside, the ranger asked, 'What do you make of it?'

'I honestly don't know,' I answered.

He shook his head as he folded up the paper and I made the tisking sound that decent and bewildered Americans made in sympathy, all of us feeling the world was changing too fast.

IT WAS A very different place we found when we parked our Valiant in front of the tall Victorian house. The porch—we used to sit out on it in broken chairs—was swept clean, barren of chairs, as if no one sat out anymore to watch the neighbors. After we rang the bell, we waited a long time, staring at the wooden door with its oval of glass. When it opened, Aunt Katherine stood there, bent over a cane.

'Girls,' she said, 'I'm so glad you've come.' She led us into the living room and slowly lowered herself onto a sofa. Doris and I stood, looking around at the oil paintings, the stuffed deer's head, everything that had enchanted us as children.

'Is that the girls?' Letty walked in, wiping her hands on her apron; she seemed thinner and withered, her skin not as black. Suddenly a memory came back to me: Letty sitting down with a sigh and telling us about the sailor she loved. 'He'd pick me up in those arms and swing me around.' Poor Letty's sailor was killed in the war.

Now Letty stood next to Aunt Katherine's chair, her hand resting just behind Aunt Katherine's head. I could see from the way she stood so close how things were. Letty wasn't a cook and Aunt Katherine wasn't her employer so much as they were two old spinsters living together, two women made level by loneliness.

*

WHEN LETTY AND Doris disappeared to fix us some lunch, I searched for my father among the framed photographs that sat in rows on top of the piano, like tombstones.

'On the end, dear,' Aunt Katherine said.

I picked up the silver frame tentatively. He looked so young in the sepia photo—bespectacled, curly hair cropped short, thin lips clamped. 'Would you mind very much if I kept this?' I asked.

'It should be yours,' she said.

I sat down beside her on the sofa. 'It's strange to see him young.'

She took the picture, her gnarled fingers next to his smooth face. 'I remember that summer you were here, oh, that was a hard time for him. He'd just gotten out of the C.P.S, and I don't think he was ever the same.'

Our father was a man who would not go to war. He never told me how, exactly, he'd come to his convictions; I wish now I'd asked him. I know he went to socialist meetings in college, where it was widely understood among the young men that World War I had been a plot of international bankers. And so, during his war, the Second World War, he registered as a conscientious objector; since his mother had been Quaker, Dad pleaded for C.O. status on religious grounds and was given it. People think he had it easy while other men fought and died, but the truth is, Dad dug ditches ten hours a day, and on top of that drank sea water for months as part of a medical experiment. But he did not come back a hero; no, people in our town called him a communist or a coward. This picture showed him before the war, perhaps when he was still at the university.

'Aunt Katherine?' I asked. She gazed up at me, her eyes milky. Though she sat near enough that I could smell her faint odor of old tea, I felt she was far away, farther even than my father. It was there I longed to be too—in the comforting cocoon of an old maid's life.

I said, 'Do you remember what Mom and Dad were like the summer we visited?'

'Oh, I remember,' she said. 'I'll never forget your lovely mother. But your father, as I said, he was troubled. He barely talked, and I remember how we all worried about him.' She laid her cool, crooked hand on my arm and we said no more about it.

That evening, Letty showed me my room. It had a white bedspread woven with a raised pattern; a high, stately chest of drawers, like a disapproving gentleman; and an engraving of a horse with an accusing eye. Letty left, and for the first time I was alone with the picture of my father. The frame was of tarnished silver covered with intricate scollwork. The back side was upholstered with faded green velvet, which, when stroked, sent up tendrils of dust. Little pegs like nails held the velvet backing to the frame.

Ashamed of what I was about to do, I shut the door. Then I pried those pegs out of their holes like tiny nails from a tiny coffin, and slipped my father from his frame. The photograph was decomposing, turning into powder in my fingers like a butterfly wing. I held it up to the light of the window, peering at the hairs of his eyebrows, the rococo folds of his ear, the perfect curve of his cheek. What was he thinking, just at the moment when the picture was snapped? I stared into his remote eyes for several minutes, until I heard Doris walking up the stairs. Hastily, I hid the picture and frame in a drawer. A minute later, I came to my senses: I couldn't fathom why I had taken the picture out when I knew touching it would only hasten its decay.

AFTER A FEW days, we fell into Aunt Katherine's and Letty's rhythm. In the morning, Letty brought us cereal in bowls and a crystal pitcher of milk. Some afternoons, she or Aunt Katherine would give us a grocery list, and we'd drive the Valiant over to the store.

Letty still made her fabulous dinners: biscuits that left white circles of flour on your fingers, raspberry jam in a silver dish, glistening pot roasts, mashed sweet potatoes studded with walnuts, pecan pie with a crust that crumbled at the touch of a fork.

Afterward, we all sat around the TV for the news. For three years our cities had been burning, and now it seemed every Negro we saw on the news raised a fist or spit out angry words. I snuck glances at Letty, suddenly embarrassed by my whiteness and her blackness. I expected her to say something about the riots—something to comfort the rest of us, perhaps—but she just kept on rocking. In her lap she held a paper fan with garish reproduction of the Last Supper on it.

I don't think she paid any attention to the TV. Neither did Aunt Katherine, who sat with her head bent, her hand cocked on her cane. Sometimes they talked to each other while the TV was on— about how Cousin Lilah, long dead, had looked in her wedding dress, or the summer when the house flooded. In their presence, I too began to lose interest in the confusing tangle of hatreds we saw on TV.

DORIS AND I occupied the top half of the house, rooms with strange, unwanted pieces of furniture in them, where we walked along the dark corridors like ghosts.

I was quick to learn the arts of spinster-hood. I pulled back lacy curtains to watch the street below; I gazed at pinpricks of dust as they meandered in the sunlight; I knitted out the minutes, turning time into knots of yarn; I saved paper bags, folding them into squares and tying them up with bits of twine.

Even as a girl I had wanted to be an old maid—probably because Mom's life seemed so disagreeable. She'd sit at the sewing machine, trying to hurry a hem, and then her pot would begin boiling over, the lid chattering to itself, and she'd jump up and run to the kitchen, and then the phone would start ringing—the grocer wanting her to pay the bill or some such. She might sit down for a moment to improve her mind with the *Saturday Evening Post*, but soon enough she would jump up again and disappear into the kitchen, where I'd hear her loudly whisper, 'Darn it, darn it, darn it,' as she tried to light the stove.

In contrast to my hurried and harried mother were the spinsters: Aunt Katherine and Letty, Miss Land our piano teacher, cousin Andrea Sprats, Miss Donahue who lived down the street, and many others whom I can no longer name. They bewitched me with the muffled sounds in their houses, and their

9

candy dishes, and their private rituals ('Whenever the phone rings,' Miss Land confessed to me once, 'I try to guess who it will be. Do you do that?') I liked to imagine how they lived with so much empty time, how they, so unlike my mother, would wash each dish separately, trying to make the work last as long as possible into their empty evenings. I must have been eight or nine when I decided I wanted that kind of calm, that almost religious simplicity—though I didn't want to live alone like Miss Land. I'd be like Aunt Katherine, who had her Letty, or like my Cousin Andrea, a sagging woman who still slept in her girlhood bedroom and played Hearts every night with her parents. I never wavered from wanting that . . . No, that's not true. There were a few years during my twenties when I was in love. But he never did propose—eventually he married someone else. I was devastated, of course, though not as much as one might expect, and soon I settled back into my life with Dad and Doris, a life as comfortable as an old easy chair.

Those years before Dad died were strangely happy ones for me, I loved the quiet evenings spent with the two of them, the way we'd become so close that we lost track of where one of us ended and the others began. That's how I hoped it would be at Aunt Katherine's; Doris and I would move in here and care for the old women, and eventually the four of us would become as close as sisters. I wanted that, a cocoon of family around me.

There was only one problem—Doris. She despised idleness, and in the end that was her undoing as a spinster. When Dad had gotten too sick to keep up with his paperwork, Doris had taken over. She'd sit in his office, her reading glasses catching the light in half-moons. But now, at Aunt Katherine's, she hurried in and out of rooms, her footsteps angry. I think she missed running Dad's business; missed ushering the farmers into the darkest, coolest recesses of the warehouse and helping them to find the right tractor part; missed the old office even, with the green glass shades over the lights and high oak cabinets, the place where we'd visited Dad as children.

It wasn't but a few days until she was ready to leave—I could see it coming before she'd said anything. She swept every inch of the top two floors of the house, her broom stabbing at the dark, dusty, floor. After she finished, she walked downstairs and stood with her hands on her back, looking around for more floor to go at.

'Don't you touch the ground floor,' I whispered to her. 'That's Letty's.'

My idea was to keep Doris distracted until she settled in. 'Maybe you should get a job here,' I said, and on Sunday she humored me by looking through the help wanted.

'I suppose I could be a receptionist,' she said. She cut out the ads and tacked them up by the typewriter in the writing room upstairs.

I remembered that room from our childhood summer, because my father often cloistered himself in there. I wasn't to disturb him, but sometimes I'd kneel by the door to listen to the desultory batter of the typewriter keys. To further entertain myself, I used to gaze into the doorknob, a glass one with a silver

11

bubble inside that distorted whatever it reflected—in that bubble, I was a girl with a huge, mushroomy nose and a little body that trailed off into a thread of color. Around me, the hall warped; the window was a fingernail of light. I thought this must be how my father saw things, since his mind had gone bad during the war. I knew he was in there typing letters, explaining what had happened to him in the C.O. camps. He sent out all those letters, but only one or two newspapers ever did publish them. I suppose he seemed like a crazy man at the time. Eventually, he recovered, and worked tirelessly until he bought the business from his partners. But I believe it was then— at the age of nine—that I first began to feel that I must guard his door and to think of my father as fragile.

12

Doris never did sit down at that typewriter. The job notices stayed tacked to the cork board, fluttering whenever I opened the door to check whether she was in there. Instead, she cleaned out the linen closet, leafed through fashion magazines, lay around in her bathing suit out in the backyard, took long walks alone—and in a thousand ways broadcast to me that she did not want to be a receptionist who lived with her maiden aunt, did not want this drowsy life.

'Frannie,' she said to me one day when we were driving into town, 'I've been thinking I'll go visit Sara Hill in Richmond, do some shopping, get my hair done. I have to get out of that house for a while. I can't think in there.'

'Why, that's a good idea,' I said. 'We should both go together. Yes, we'll have to do that someday.'

I let my voice trail off to suggest that the present time was not convenient.

ONE NIGHT DORIS snapped on the TV for the news, while the rest of us sat in fat chairs, talking about maybe playing a game of bridge. We were ignoring the TV set, which like Aunt Katherine herself, was always slow to respond: a bubble of light would cautiously fill up the dull, greenish screen, and a minute later you'd get the sound.

Doris interrupted us. 'Look at this,' she said. 'What's going on?'

We watched a crush of people pushing each other, as if they were fighting to grab at the same thing, and as soon as the sound came on, we heard them screaming. When we found out it was Bobby Kennedy, Letty clapped her hand to her mouth. 'Oh Lord, oh lord,' she said. 'Not another one.'

Aunt Katherine's face was blank and bluish in the light of the TV. She blinked several times but didn't say a word.

Later I said to Doris, 'I'm just glad Dad didn't have to see this.' Our father had read the paper every morning of his life until the very end. Despite what had happened to him in the C.O. camps, he always had great faith in our country, in its Adlai Stevensons, in its liberal intellectuals, in its spiritual leaders who rose from poverty. Once I found him sitting up in bed, gently running his fingers over a newsprint picture of Dr. King. He looked up at me and said, 'Frannie, if I were only a young man, I'd be down there. I'd put myself on the line.'

'I know you would, Dad,' I'd said.

13

He died the day after Dr. King. Seven hundred fires were burning the day we laid our father in the ground.

SOON AFTER BOBBY Kennedy was shot, Letty came down with a terrible cough. We drove her to the emergency room because she scared us so, the way her frail body jerked as she hacked and hacked. The doctor handed her a bottle of pills and assured us she'd be fine, though it was nearly a month before she could laugh without it turning into a cough.

As we drove home from the hospital that day, with Letty propped up in the front seat, I couldn't help feeling triumphant: now Doris wouldn't leave us, not for a while—she would have to help Aunt Katherine, who was nearly blind, to pay her bills and answer letters. She would have to make compresses for Letty's chest.

I'm ashamed to admit how happy I was when Letty got sick. Now I'd have someone to care for again; I missed the closeness with my father, the way he depended on me. But Letty wasn't my father, no, not at all. The first time I tried to bring her breakfast, she took one look and said, 'Oh Honey, don't. I can get my own.' I knew she hated it, the way I was trying to switch places on her and become *her* servant, to coddle and nurse her as I had my father. So I let her creep down in her slippers and fix her own meals.

Aunt Katherine didn't require much attention either. I read to her, which she would tolerate for a half-hour or so before she said, 'Thank you, dear, but my head is getting tired.' She much preferred to talk—about the butcher who cheated her during the Depression ('I knew before anyone else that man was up to no good'), about the neighbors who'd once had a loud dog. I tried asking questions, I tried to get her to talk about my father and mother, what they were like, but she got annoyed with me—I suppose I was a poor substitute for Letty.

So that's how it was, me trying to turn Letty into my father and Aunt Katherine trying to turn me into Letty, and Doris gone most of the time. She'd disappear for hours and come back smelling of alcohol sometimes. I knew better than to ask where she'd been.

AFTER A FEW weeks, I had to face up to my own unhappiness. Aunt Katherine's was nothing like I'd imagined it to be. I thought I'd fall back into the quiet contentment of those years with Dad and Doris, that I'd become close with the two old women. But their past wasn't mine; they spoke a language I'd never understand. I felt like a poor relation around them, nothing but another place setting at the table, a young person they had to humor.

Yet there was more to it than that. I had begun to grow restless—maybe because of Bobby Kennedy. After he died, the whole country had gone crazy with grief. Every channel you flipped to on TV showed the same funeral, the same saluting soldiers and slow-marching processions and eternal flame. When I went into town, it was all anyone wanted to talk about—not Bobby Kennedy, exactly, but how any man you loved could be shot down.

'Wasn't he handsome, though? And now

he's gone, just like that,' the check-out girl at the supermarket said to me. 'I just don't know what's wrong with this country.'

His death made me feel wild, as if even in that shuttered-up house of Aunt Katherine's it was no good to hide from the sick-sweet smell of funeral incense, from life that can end with one crack of a gun. And so when Doris mentioned a trip to Richmond again, I said I'd like to go. We waited until Letty was her old self and then packed up our overnight bags, leaving our big suitcases on top of the beds like promises that we would be back. I must say, when we rolled out of that driveway, I didn't give that slit-windowed house so much as one backwards glance.

As soon as we pulled out onto the highway, Doris and I got into the first fight since Dad died. It was a familiar one—in many ways, the same one we'd had all our lives.

Doris, trying to get on my good side, said, 'I was just thinking about that summer we were kids at Aunt Katherine's, the day you and I climbed up onto the lifeguard chair. We were going to jump off, just like the big kids. Dad went up after us, but instead of making us climb down again, he took our hands and we all three jumped into the sand. We all came apart in the air, but when we landed he grabbed our hands again, to pretend we'd never let go.'

The minute she paused, I said, 'Doris! That wasn't here, that was in Maine.'

She tightened her grip on the wheel. She always started off being patient with me. 'It was?'

16

'And it wasn't all three of us that jumped, it was just you and Dad.'

'No, Frannie, that's not true. I remember it.' She could humor me for a while, but eventually I always dragged her into a fight. 'And you got to have a two-piece. I had that plaid one-piece, and I was walking around looking for the places where Mom stubbed out her cigarettes, and then I saw the two of you up there on the lifeguard stand. The two of you were beautiful, and I felt so ugly.'

'Frannie, stop it.'

'I just wish you'd remember it right,' I said. I always held this over her, my better memory, for I could recall the most minute details of long-ago conversations, while she liked to turn the past into stories she could tell, not necessarily true, but true-seeming.

17

Doris didn't look away from the road, but she said in a small voice, 'I swear, Fran, I don't know what's gotten into you.'

I breathed out a sigh and said, 'I'm sorry. I'm just all on edge today. You know how I get.'

Doris glanced at me, 'I know.' Then she looked ahead again and we were silent. I stared out the window at the saw grass waving on the marshy soil. Ahead a young man and woman were walking barefoot, heads down. When we passed, the shadow of our car darkened them, and I turned to catch a glimpse of their grieving faces. 'It's not just us,' I thought, 'everyone's in mourning.' And it seemed to me right and proper, now that our father was gone, to be traveling across this America widowed by war and orphaned of its great and beautiful men.

Chapter Two

WE'D LIVED IN a small New Hampshire town where everyone knew us. For instance, when we went to the Band Box luncheonette, Lorna would stand over our table and ask, 'Egg salads for you two?'—and before we could answer she'd lean into the kitchen and say, 'Petey, make up some egg salads for the sisters.' That's how small our town was: everyone knew your name and what you liked for lunch, too. But now we sat in a diner with a view of the highway and the eighteen-wheelers parked out front. We hadn't really needed to stop, but turning off to go to a diner was a treat—one of the enticements Doris had promised me.

Our waitress looked past us dully as we ordered, scribbling on her pad. When she left, I leaned forward and whispered, 'She didn't even know what we wanted—we're very mysterious women!' I meant that here among the truckers with their obscene arm muscles, the families headed for the beach with children clutching sand buckets, and the two regulars sitting at the counter talking with the cook, no one could guess our story.

'Of course they can tell who we are, what kind of people we are—it's plain as day.' Doris stirred her coffee in graceful circles. She had her hair up and was wearing a white shirt with a Peter Pan collar. I could still see the creases where it had been ironed. Clothes hung on her loosely like that, and me as well—though she looked elegant and lean, whereas I just looked skinny. I was only in my mid-thirties, but I'd already achieved the pinched look of a woman who reuses her teabags and keeps her pennies in a tight little purse.

I was about to say something to Doris when our table lurched, sending concentric circles rippling through the coffee; I heard a throat clearing and a thrumming click. A man stood over us, still holding the fancy camera up to his face.

I scowled at him. 'Please,' I said, 'we're trying to eat.' Instead of leaving, he lowered the camera and stuck out his hand so I had to shake it. 'Richard,' he said. 'I'm sorry if I disturbed you.'

I took an immediate dislike to him because he was so handsome. Though he was somewhere in his forties, he was still trim. His hair, brown with flecks of gray in it, was too long for my taste. He wore a button-down shirt and jeans. What made him so handsome, I suppose, were his high cheekbones and the unnatural silvery blue of his eyes.

Doris laughed. 'Heavens, why would you want our picture?'

He crossed his arms and regarded us for a minute. 'Well,' he said, 'I take pictures of just about everything. But, you know, I was sitting at that table there reading the paper and then I caught sight of you two talking. You were hunched toward each other in such a strange way, which made me think, "They have some kind of secret." So I wanted to catch that.'

'We're sisters,' Doris said, as if that explained it. She didn't seem to mind him, but I thought him terribly queer. 'Are you a professional photographer?' she asked.

'I teach photography at a college near here.' And then, as if to prove that he was a professor, he took a pipe out of his pocket and put it in his mouth, making a great show of lighting it. 'I also run a bed and breakfast. Don't have any guests right now, though. Summer's a bad season—too hot.'

There was something so masculine about him that I felt uncomfortably aware of my own, of Doris's femininity. Suddenly I was conscious again—as I had always been during high school—that she was the prettier one. Oh, how I remembered sitting in diners like this one, while the boys talked up Doris as if I wasn't there.

When his pipe was lit, he asked us the usual questions. It came out that our father had just died, but he did not seem embarrassed. Instead he said, 'Hmm, maybe that's why you two had that secretive look.'

Doris seemed confused by his bluntness. She said, 'We're still mourning him.'

He nodded, as if he already knew our whole story. Suddenly, he reminded me of one of our father's suppliers, who used to visit our house, a man whom I loathed. I still remembered him saying to me, a teenager, 'Eat bananas, Frannie, and that skin will clear up.' Now, in my mind, this man became that one.

The conversation turned again to his photographs, and he said, 'If you have some time, I'll show them to you. You should see the place, too.'

DORIS DROVE. I sat with my fists in my lap. 'What has gotten into you?' I said.

As always in arguments, she remained calm. 'Now, Frannie, he seems very nice.'

'Well, I don't like him,' I said. 'We don't know a thing about him. How do you know this is safe?'

'Look him up,' she said. 'Look him up in the Esso guide.'

I sorted through the maps in the glove compartment until I found it—*The Esso Guide to the American Highway*, with the bed and breakfasts listed in the back. 'He's here,' I said wearily. 'The address he gave us.'

'You see,' she said, 'it's official. He's harmless.'

'Oh come on, Doris. I'll just bet he wants to show us his photographs. That's the oldest line in the world.'

'How would you know?' she asked.

'I read about artists in *Life* magazine.' I watched Richard's black Dodge ahead of us—the outline of his head like a shadow in its rear window—and thought how it was all starting again.

21

When we were little, Doris and I had been inseparable. We marched to school in matching outfits, and, when other children walked by, we began talking in our own secret language. But in high school, one year's growth spurt turned her into a tall, auburn-haired beauty. That summer, she sat in our bedroom with her chin on her knees. I'd peer around her door and say, 'Doris, come on downstairs,' and she'd lift her head to look at me absent-mindedly, and say, 'No thanks.' She'd always had a few friends in school, quiet, bookish girls; but when that year began—ninth grade for her, seventh for me—she fell in with the popular girls, all blonde and giggly. I'd see her walk down the hall arm-in-arm with them, laughing. At home, though, she was silent, staring out windows and meandering in and out of rooms, trailing her hand along the wall. Things only got worse. She went on dates, running out the door with her coat half on. If she talked to me at all, it was to ask how a necklace looked with a dress, whether her shoes were right.

Then, when she was seventeen, our mother died—a car, speeding down a lonely road, that never stopped—and I had the bitter pleasure of Doris being mine again. For the next twenty years, we read to each other, cooked together, and when Dad began his long decline, nursed him. She still went out on dates, though it was different: I knew she wouldn't leave us.

But now I realized that, with Dad gone, there was nothing to keep Doris from leaving me.

RICHARD PULLED UP in front of a farmhouse shaded by old trees. Doris was ignoring me. She got out of the car and stretched, closing her eyes and smiling. He ambled over, his boots crunching on the gravel. 'Not too long a drive, I hope?'

'A lovely drive,' she said. With dread I recognized the bubbly high school Doris.

I tried to be pleasant. 'What grand old trees.' He turned his eyes on me. It was perhaps their strange color alone that made me feel I had said something foolish.

'Come on in,' he said, and opened the door for us. As he led us down a dark hallway, I trailed behind. I was cursing Doris for her foolish trust in strangers. *He could hack us into pieces*, I thought. *He could be a murderer*. I entertained this idea only because I was in the habit of thinking sensible thoughts; I wasn't really afraid of Richard. The truth was, Doris had a good eye for strangers; it was I who might have gotten us in trouble, since I often mistook the thinnest patina of politeness for a sterling soul.

23

We entered a room all a mess with cords, tripods and curling photographs that hung on the walls every which way. There was a sharp stench of chemicals.

'These are the ones I've just finished,' he said and sat down. Doris and I walked around the room, leaning close to each photograph.

'What do you think, honestly?' He said it as if it didn't matter, his arms crossed, one hand holding his pipe—but I could see by the way his eyes fastened on me and then Doris that it mattered terribly.

'I don't know much about art . . .' Doris said. 'But I think they're the most wonderful pictures I've ever seen.'

They actually did seem to be quite good. I remember one of a boy wearing a black cape, another simply of a white curtain billowing.

'They're like things from dreams,' I said.

He smiled at me. 'Yes,' he said. For a minute it seemed we understood one another.

He invited us into his kitchen for coffee, which he made in a strange contraption on the stove, so it came out strong and bitter. The house was the darnedest thing I'd ever seen; I didn't know how he expected anyone to *pay* to stay there. Every stick of his furniture seemed about to fall apart: a sofa swathed in an Indian tapestry, sagging chairs, rugs with white circles of wear in them and beaded curtains that hung where there should have been doors. It was then that I missed our own furniture: the straight-backed chairs and solid little tables shaped like teacakes. They were probably all getting moldy where we had stored them down in the basement.

Doris ran her finger around the rim of her cup. 'I think it's terribly exciting—your life. Tell me, do you live alone—I mean, when there aren't any guests?' She kept her head bent, but raised her eyes to look at him.

'No, not really. I have friends—disreputable artist types—who come and stay for free. Otherwise it gets a bit lonely sometimes.' He took a sip from his coffee, and then carefully put it on the table. 'Right now, Mim is here. She's from Czechoslovakia.'

'*Oho!*' I thought.

He said, 'I like to have people come out here and stay, especially when school's out.'

*

WE STAYED. IT started with Doris saying, in that false voice of hers, 'What do people do when they come here—you know, the attractions?'

Richard listed them as he stood at the stove, making more coffee: a boardwalk amusement park, a beach, woods, a nearby mountain to climb.

'That sounds *much* better than Richmond, don't you think?' she said to me coyly. 'Wouldn't it be fun to stay for a night, Frannie?'

'Of course it would,' I said politely. 'But you know we're expected.'

'Well, I can fix that easily enough,' she said—then, to Richard, 'You don't mind, do you?'

'I'd love it,' he said. 'There's no one coming until next week.'

'Wonderful, then it's settled.'

And so it went, before I could say another word. Doris knew just how to trap me in my own etiquette: no matter how little I wanted to stay, I wouldn't dare say anything in front of Richard.

After the coffee, he showed us to adjoining bedrooms. 'There's something about these that suits you two,' he said. I could see what he meant. The rooms were old-fashioned, with dark floors, high beds, eccentric night tables, and squat little lamps with dotted shades. Each room had a window filled with the shifting green shade of the old tree outside. All of a sudden, I saw the house as it had been once: a large family had lived here, with the two eldest daughters in these rooms. Those girls were frail old women now.

Doris and I, too, had shared a room like these when we were children. Such rooms are all of a kind: comfortingly dark and musty, smelling of moth-balls, quiet as tombs. As a little girl, you get sick in such a room and lie for hours looking at the pattern of roses on the curtains until your mother comes in and pours medicine into a spoon and puts her cool hand across your forehead. In such a room, you are always in some way a sick child waiting for your mother to come upstairs.

Richard said he'd like to take a walk—it was getting to be evening now, and much cooler out. Would we come? Doris would, of course, but I said I was too tired. I didn't want to see it: she touching his arm to draw his attention or laughing too long at his jokes.

I sat on my bed a long time, hands folded in my lap. Mostly, I suppose, I looked out the window. In any other mood, I would have found the view beautiful. Beyond the old tree was an overgrown field dusted with white flowers, and behind that, a post-card-blue sky. But the field seemed desolate; the flowers bobbed feebly. I felt it then: something was going to happen. Something was going to change. And the sun fell across the dark floor, just as it had in the house where I grew up, and I imagined Dad in his room down the hall, dying with the same patient slowness as a square of sunlight that creeps across the carpet.

THE DOOR SLAMMED. 'Hello, Richard?' a woman called in a thick accent. I considered not saying anything, but the old pull of politeness got me on my feet and into the living room.

'Hello,' I said.

She spun around, smiling. 'Oh, hi. You a friend of Richard's?' She was older than I expected: my age, I might even have guessed, though she was taller and of a heavier, heartier build than I. Her blonde hair was piled up above her face, and despite the heat, she wore a short velvet dress and black tights.

I introduced myself and said, 'Richard took our picture today, and now he and my sister are on a walk.'

'I'm Mim.' She had a way of staring unblinkingly into my face as she spoke that made me nervous. 'We'll make dinner, OK?' she said.

We stood at a counter—she peeling and chopping vegetables, and I scrubbing the pots, which had been hanging on the wall as if they were clean, though they weren't at all.

'Richard says you're Czech.'

'Yeah, sure thing,' she said, then put her knife down and began searching through the cabinets. 'I left a few months ago, when I could still get out. I knew Richard through my brother, also a photographer, so I came here.'

I asked about her family, but she turned her back to me and said, 'I know what,' and pulled down a bottle of something green.

She poured it into two ruby-colored glasses, held one glass to her lips, and closed her eyes while she drained it—and kept her eyes closed for a long time afterward. It was a revelation to me, the way she enjoyed it. I had to hold my glass a long time, afraid to take a sip, because then it would be gone, the

27

emerald drink that smelled of mint, the way my mother had.

'There's more, go, drink up,' Mim said, but still I held the drink up to the light, sniffed it, took the tiniest sips and thus rationed out the glassful.

Even as a child I had been like that. When we came home from school, our mother would hand us each a cookie. Doris ate hers as she ran up the stairs to our room, but I saved mine until after my homework. That was the secret to pleasure, I thought: keep it always in the future. Later I began saving the cookies until bedtime, and after that, keeping them in shoeboxes, afraid to eat them at all.

Mim laughed at me. 'We have to cook.' She stood with her arms crossed. 'Drink it!'

I did, and then, intoxicated—for I never drank, as a rule—I helped her spice the stew, cut the black bread and lay the table.

WHEN THEY WALKED into the living room, they were laughing. Doris's cheeks were flushed, and she had a distracted look, the same I'd seen in high school, when she and her friends walked past me.

Richard hugged Mim. 'How's it going?'

She sighed. 'Richard, I am so behind.'

He smiled at her—mysteriously, tenderly— and said, 'You just like to complain about it. You know you always finish early.'

He leaned over the table, ripped off a piece of bread and took a bite. 'I guess you've met Frannie,' he said, pointing to my sister with the piece of bread. 'This is Dorie.'

I turned to fiddle with something on the table so they would not see my face. I hadn't heard that name since before our mother died. The boys who called had asked for 'Dorie,' and when I handed her the receiver, she'd stare at me until I left our room. I'd wander down to the living room to sit beside my father as he read, his fingers lingering on the pages as he turned them, unaware of the faint buzz of her phone conversation upstairs—a sound as constant in our house as the hum of the Frigidaire.

LATER THAT EVENING, I stood in Doris's room, watching as she hung up her clothes. Finally, I said, 'I don't want to see you get hurt.'

She laughed in little gusts of breath, 'Oh dear me, Frannie, don't be so melodramatic.'

'But the way he's leading you on. I can't stand to see it.'

'When did he lead me on? Just give me one example,' she said, leaning over her suitcase as she sorted through whispering linens.

'You just tell me what he's doing living here with that woman.'

'I know exactly what he's doing, because I asked'—and then she smoothed out a dress on the bed and turned from me to hang it up.

'What?'

'Never you mind. It would just upset you.' I felt frozen. I heard myself saying, 'We have to leave right away.'

She leaned toward her suitcase again. 'Don't be ridiculous,' she said. 'There's nothing wrong with them. It's *us* that's strange, not them.'

'I see it coming,' I said. 'Something terrible is going to happen. We have to leave.'

Doris slammed her suitcase shut. It bounced open again slightly. I restrained myself from going over and tucking in clothing so that the suitcase would close properly. She said, 'Frannie, you can't have me all to yourself. Honestly, you hate it when I have fun.' It was true, I thought self-righteously: I did hate it when she had fun with people I could see would use her, people we didn't know from Adam. But instead of saying this, I turned and walked out of the room. It was the first time we had parted angrily in years.

WHEN I GOT up the next morning, everyone was already in the kitchen. Doris was at the stove, flipping pancakes. Then, like a slap, I remembered it was Sunday: pancakes had always been our Sunday treat for Dad.

They had already decided we would go to the beach, so after breakfast we piled into the Valiant. I still hadn't made up with Doris, who was driving, her arm cocked out the window. Strands of hair had come loose from her bun and twitched all around her head like live wires.

We parked by the boardwalk and strolled out into the dunes. Mim held her loose cotton dress up above her pale knees and waded into the water. 'Hey, you guys, come in,' she yelled, closing her eyes and smiling. She scooped up some water and poured it on her head. Richard—in shorts and a T-shirt—waded after her. Doris held his camera. She and I stood on a wooden walkway that ended in sand. Since

30

we hadn't packed any outfits for the beach, we both wore crisp, white shirts, narrow skirts, stockings, and pumps.

All around us were teenagers—girls in bikinis and long-haired boys with surfboards. Where were the families, the elderly ladies I remembered from our childhood days at the beach? Something had happened all those years that Doris and I were shut up in the house: the whole world had grown young.

After Mim and Richard's dip, we all walked along the boardwalk. Doris and I fell into step. 'Smell that tar,' she said. 'Sure brings it all back . . .' It was her way of making up, I suppose. We began talking of the boardwalk of our childhood—freak show tents, screams above us from people riding a rickety roller-coaster, sailors with smooth, evil faces, drunks lying on the sand curled around their bottles—all of it so wonderful to us.

I turned and saw Richard was walking close behind us, listening. 'I'm sorry,' he laughed, 'I shouldn't eavesdrop.'

'Frannie and I were just remembering the good old days,' Doris said.

'So that's the secret between you—a happy childhood.' He was smiling, but when he looked at me his eyes were so pale—like the white eyes of statues—that I felt he was seeing inside me.

'Depends who you ask,' Doris said. 'Frannie was happy. Personally, I couldn't wait until it was over.' She fell into step with Richard, and they began talking and laughing between themselves; I trailed behind and had to make conversation with Mim.

After lunch, we rented folding chairs and

sat on the beach. Mim fiddled with her radio until she found a station that was playing big band music.

'I've been teaching Richard to dance!' she said. 'He's not quite as dreadful anymore.' She held out her hand to him, and they waltzed on the sand; sometimes the waves ran up around their ankles. They were laughing, Mim's sand-colored hair blowing all around them.

'Why, just look at that, Frannie,' Doris said. She was sitting beside me in her beach chair. 'They seem to be having so much fun.'

'I think they just want everyone to look at them—you know, to show off.'

But Doris wasn't even listening to me. Slowly, she stood up, pulled her skirt straight, and peeled off her pumps, which she arranged side by side in front of her chair. In her stocking feet, she walked away from me. Mim and Richard broke apart, and the three of them talked. Then Doris and Richard embraced, and awkwardly began to dance. Mim stood by, laughing, shouting directions.

The breeze lifted, blowing sand against my skin, and soon I couldn't hear them anymore. They were waltzing away from me. Beside me sat Doris's pumps, primly together. There, on the sand, they looked like two empty shells.

Chapter Three

I DON'T KNOW how it happened, exactly, but days went by at Richard's. There was always something else Doris just had to see—a shipping museum, a picnic spot—and when I complained, she said, 'Well, you could always take the car and go, and I'll just hop on the bus when I'm ready to leave.' Of course, she knew I wouldn't do that. And so, just like when we were teenagers, I became Doris's appendage, her sullen and resentful companion.

One day she insisted we drive to the department store in a nearby town. She'd suddenly decided that she needed new dresses. When I reminded her that we had plenty of clean clothes back at Aunt Katherine's, she said, 'I can't stand the thought of wearing those little dress suits anymore,' with a mysterious flick of her tongue across her top lip. 'I'm just tired of looking like someone's maiden aunt.'

And so I found myself trailing behind her,

my reflection swirling across the glass of the revolving door as it sucked me in and spit me into the department store, a new world of dead-eyed mannequins and little crumpled underthings hanging on racks.

Oh, it might seem like something that happens every day, two women going shopping at a department store. But I was entering enemy territory: I don't think I'd ever been inside a department store in my life. The poor people in our town shopped at Heckingers and J. C. Penney, and I always considered it beneath me.

Where had Doris and I bought our clothes? There was a ladies' shop over in Keene, a place of the white-gloves-and-two-piece-suit persuasion, with a saleslady whose hair was stiff as seven-minute icing. She'd always been there by my reckoning, or at least since my mother brought us to the store as girls. Years later, whenever I insisted on making the pilgrimage to Keene for new clothes, Doris threw a fit. 'We're not going to that nasty place with the old bat, are we?' she'd demand. 'That woman walks in on me when I'm changing, like I'm still ten years old.' But I'd managed to instill Doris with my own fear of modern stores, of polyester blends and bad seams, so she too couldn't imagine a place where they didn't tailor your shirts for you and send them a week later, where the cottons weren't as brittle as the finest writing paper.

And so, I followed Doris through the department store, marveling at the strangeness of everything around me. The place was as large as a warehouse, with linoleum floors that squeaked under my shoes. Here and there, mannequins had been posed together, like mysterious creche scenes. Everything seemed hopelessly garish and cheap; and, to my mind, the perfumey smell of those clothes we passed was a scent of sin.

Doris walked through the store as if she'd done it a million times, past the matronly gray dresses, up an escalator and underneath a sign that said SOCK IT TO ME in pink letters. Soon she stood before the mirror in a sleeveless black shift, her long, white arms exposed, her hair unpinned so it fell past her shoulders.

'Doris, that dress is too young for you,' I said. 'Do you really want to parade around like that?'

'I'm not going to even credit that with an answer,' she snapped, so I didn't say anything more, even about all the money she was wasting. Of course, with the income from dad's store and the house, we had a good sum coming in every month—but how long would it last?

When we walked outside, she was wearing the black dress, sandals, and sunglasses. I felt I was suddenly in the company of a foreigner. In her new clothes, she said little and moved her arms with as much grace as if she were wearing long white gloves.

'It's Richard, isn't it?' I said. 'You want new clothes so he'll notice you.'

She sighed as she slid into the driver's seat. 'Oh, grow up, Frannie.'

Silently, Doris adjusted the mirror and started up the engine. The car, loaded with all those packages sprouting tissue, was filled with the cloying scent of the department store. She glanced behind as she backed out of the parking space, and I caught a flash of my reflection in her sunglasses; I looked like a

35

ghost, a faint line of white sliding over the black plastic.

'It's not fair,' I thought. 'She shouldn't have spent all that money.' But really I was thinking—though I wouldn't admit it to myself—how lovely it would be to wear a loose dress, to sprawl, to loll, and still to look as beautiful as she did.

When we got back to Richard's, she went out to the shed and found herself a lawn chair. I watched from the window as she carried a fashion magazine and the chair out into the front yard, and sat almost invisible in the high grass. No doubt she was reading about hairlines or hemlines, about fresh-looking skin or long legs.

And I sat in that window and watched her run her finger down the pages of that magazine, sure that she was waiting for Richard's car.

THERE'S A SUMMER I return to again and again, when my mother always seemed to be crouched in the garden, picking bugs off of leaves and dropping them into a can of kerosine. She called the little plot of land behind our patio her 'victory garden.' I never understood why, because her mood—when she came into the house, dirt on the knees of her slacks—was one of defeat. 'It's terrible, Frannie,' she'd say. 'All the tomatoes are dead.'

I liked to spy on her from my room as she worked in the garden. I would perch on my window-sill two stories up, sometimes stringing beads, sometimes sewing a dress for my doll; sometimes I'd lean out, with one foot on the roof, to get a better view of her. The sun made a circle of light on her hair, which was brushed tightly into a bun. She would kneel in the dirt, shaking her head as if she wanted to cry. She'd pick something off a plant, hold it carefully in her gloved hand, and then drop it into the can.

That summer, Doris was staying at Uncle Jack's house in Texas, and I had our room all to myself. I sprawled across her bed to read. I went through the drawer in which she kept Bazooka wrappers, movie ticket stubs, marbles, and Crackerjacks prizes. Underneath these, in a ring box that snapped shut like a trap, I found her baby teeth—they were yellowed, smelled perfumey from their long habitation in the box, and were so smooth that I liked to rub them against my cheeks.

Later I grew bold enough to try on Doris's dresses. They sagged on me, the hems falling below my calves. Sometimes I'd open her closet just to run my hands along the stiff cottons, which smelled of Ivory soap, knowing that when she came back, her dresses would be tracked by my touches, an invisible net I had woven all around her.

My mother often apologized that I had not been able to go to Uncle Jack's, too. 'We couldn't saddle them with both you girls,' she said. 'Of course, if I'd had my druthers, we'd send you two off to some lovely camp.' But she didn't have her druthers; this was during the years of our desperation. My father was off serving in the CPS as a conscientious objector; for a while, on top of everything else, he suffered as a guinea pig in their medical experiments and was too sick to write letters.

During those years when the war deprived us of meat and sugar, as well as of our father, we lived in poverty. The government refused to pay the C.O.s—who, it was thought, were already getting off easy. On the coldest nights in winter, my mother used wood for heat, and the three of us slept in the living room, near the fireplace. I believe my mother asked Uncle Jack and her other relatives for help during that time, too. At any rate, we always got lavish but practical gifts from them at Christmas— coats and wool sweaters and even Liberty Bonds sometimes, perhaps an admonition that we should be more patriotic.

My mother never worked. Of course, she had the two of us to mind, but still, through all of our poverty, I don't believe she ever thought of getting a job. It was inconceivable that she should work. Mom was soft-spoken, anemic, and always on the verge of tears, it seemed, but a heroic woman in her way. She did everything she could to soften the grind of poverty for us, making us dresses and cooking everything from scratch.

She rationed out cigarettes to herself, saying, 'This is my last one today, girls.'

When the war board itself began rationing cigarettes, the only brand she could find was Fleet-woods. I remember her in the darkened living room, crying, a cigarette still smoking in one hand. She had looked up at me as if I were perfectly capable of understanding, and she said, 'These taste like saw-dust. I don't think there's a flake of tobacco in them,' and then broke down in another fit of tears.

Though that summer shouldn't have been one of my best, I remember it just that way. Doris and Dad were gone and my mother doted on me. She cut the crusts off my sandwiches, played Go Fish, and squandered some of the precious, rationed gasoline to drive me to a nearby lake. She'd lie on the dock while I dove into the water, feeling its slap of cold all over. I remember my languorous happiness as I dog-paddled back and forth through the quivering reflections of trees which lay on the water's surface. My mother would lift one hand to hold a stunningly white cigarette, and when she was finished with it, would throw the butt into the lake, where it landed with a sigh. I made a big show of splashing in the water and singing to myself to cover how I was sneaking glances at her. She lay on the slate-blue dock, unaware of the tendrils of slime that clung to the dock's underside, hanging down like matted hair, undulating with the tide.

At night, we sat on the front porch and she drank. I am trying to remember her as she looked then, but she is only a blur—a slip of pink against the railing, the clinking of ice, a cloud of cigarette smoke—in my memory. Sometimes, if she seemed to be in the right mood, I'd ask her when Dad was coming back for a visit, and she'd tell me how many weeks we had.

This is what I remember: the cool metal of the porch chair under my rump and the constant batter of the bugs against the lightbulb, like the sound of rain. 'Don't they ever get tired?' I asked her once.

'No,' she said, as if herself quite exhausted. 'Never, ever, ever.'

WHY IS THAT one summer so important? Why do I dwell there, forever, in some part of my mind?

What are the dark pleasures of that summer that bring me back? I think it was then, that year, amid the deprivation of the war, that I fully became Frannie. Watching my mother go through the handkerchiefs in Dad's drawer, occasionally holding one to her face to catch the fading smell of him—that's how I learned to do the same with Doris's things. My mother, wordlessly watching out the window; my mother, polishing his long-unused cufflinks with a superstitious hope, perhaps; my mother, standing in the doorway watching him read with her hungry eyes—it was she who taught me the deliciousness of obsession. My mother understood longing better than love; even when my father was home in his place, adorning his side of the living room couch, she seemed to pine for him.

Now, thinking back, I can only wonder whether he was unfaithful to her—whether it was not just the war that took him away. Was I learning how, with the precocious mimickry of a ten year old, to be a wronged woman too? Or is that too simple an explanation for how I became myself, with my constant need not to love other people but to clutch at them, to grasp and never let go?

I SAT BY the window all that afternoon and watched Doris out on the lawn. Mim had left the day before. She worked as a translator and—as if she sensed an attraction between Richard and Doris that she would do nothing to thwart—had announced that she was going to pick up her manuscript in Washington, D.C., and would stay with a friend for a few days. We'd seen her off at the train station, where she kissed us all on the cheek, leaving a perfume of tea rose.

At evening, the shadows lengthened across the lawn, the shadow of Doris crawling toward me as I stood at the window. When Richard's car came crunching up the gravel driveway, her head snapped up. He parked near her, stepped out stiffly, lifted his tripods from the back seat, and walked over to her. He laughed and said something when he saw her, then kneeled down to finger her new dress.

A few minutes later they came inside. 'Doesn't Doris look great?' he said to me.

'I liked her better before,' I said, sulking. At dinner Doris announced, in that cheerful voice she never used with me, 'I'd like to go somewhere. Not just a movie, but a neighborhood bar or something. Local color.' And I knew her intention was to get him drunk, maybe to get *herself* drunk.

'There's not much going on around here in the summer,' he said, 'but we'll see what we can do.'

'I think I'll stay in,' I said.

'No, Fran, you've got to come. What will you do here?' Doris said.

'That's right,' Richard added. 'We'll feel terrible leaving you.'

What could I do? I didn't have the gumption to argue, so I soon found myself following them to Richard's car. It was dark out, but still quite humid; the sound of the bugs, like a constant creaking, and the shifting of the trees overhead saddened me as she opened the car door to sit beside him up front.

I DIDN'T LIKE the place at all, but to my relief, it was rather empty—only the bartender and a

41

few teenagers. The walls were painted in swirls of neon color and the jukebox played pounding rock music.

'Isn't this amazing,' Doris whispered. 'I've heard about the discotheques where all the young people like to go, and here I am right in the middle of one.'

We sat at a wobbly table and the bartender, his long hair back in a pony tail, brought us drinks: whiskeys for them and a Coke for me.

'Now tell me, Richard, who are these people. What do they do for a living? Do you know them?' she said.

He made an effort to include me, looking from one of us to the other as he talked, all the while puffing on his pipe. 'My students come here,' he said. 'We all go after class once in a while. Sometimes there's a band.' He went on about his students, until Doris interrupted him.

'Excuse me,' she said, 'I'll be right back.' She got up, taking her purse.

Richard said, in a sort of stage whisper, 'What do you suppose she's up to?' For a moment it seemed we were in league, he and I, to learn my sister's mysteries. Together we watched as she, in her stranger's clothes, walked past the bathrooms, past the payphone, to the cigarette machine. She fed it with coins, ran her fingers over the knobs, and finally pulled one.

'But she doesn't smoke!' I said.

Doris came back to the table and used Richard's matches to light up. She inhaled without coughing, her puffs ladylike and practiced. I noticed

then that she had bought the same brand—Kools—
that our mother had favored.

'Doris, what has gotten into you?' I said.
She exhaled a plume of smoke that smelled of mint.
How I remembered that smell: it clung to our mother's clothes; it followed her like a ghost, so that she
left her scent on the phone receiver, the living room
sofa, on my skin.

Doris said, 'Seeing Richard smoke his pipe
made me want a drag. I used to sneak Mom's, you
know. Only now and then so she wouldn't notice. I'd
go out on the patio and prance around with the
cigarette in my hand, pretending I was a grown-up.
And here I am, a grown-up, more or less.'

The bartender came back and Richard and
Doris ordered whiskeys again. I was surprised at how
quickly they drew further and further away from me
in a slur of laughter and smoking and slapping their
hands on the table. Meanwhile, the place had begun
to fill up with scruffy-looking boys, girls in short
skirts who grabbed each others' shoulders and gig-
gled—something I remembered Doris and her friends
doing long ago. After a few hours, there was such a
crush of teenagers that they sometimes leaned against
our table, or brushed against me without apology.

Doris stood again and walked over to a boy
leaning against the jukebox. Richard laughed and
shouted over the music, 'She's up to something.' We
watched her talk to the boy and then put her dime in
the machine and press the buttons. Richard smiled at
me awkwardly. 'A cigarette and a song,' he said,
setting down his drink—by now his fifth—so it
sloshed over the sides of the glass.

43

Doris came back to the table and grabbed him by the arm. 'Come on,' she said. She led him to the jukebox and leaned over it, pointing, her face lit from below by the purple glow of the machine. With the next song—a slow one—she and Richard began a waltz. The kids made room, some laughing at them, as Richard and Doris stomped unsteadily in circles.

Alone at that table, I suddenly felt lost, overcome by a great weariness. I held my hands over my ears, closed my eyes and pictured our town as it would be now, the gingerbread houses glowing white against the fine sky, each with an American flag hanging in front, floating on the breeze. After a sudden New Hampshire thunderstorm, the road would be dotted with puddles reflecting webs of branches or swatches of blue sky. Our town itself was really no more than one long street lined with old factories and stores; driving toward that street from the side, you could see how hills rose straight up behind the blackened brick buildings. And our house—that's what I missed most of all. I pictured myself standing on the dirt road, looking through the trees at our mossy, three-story Victorian, which was flanked by purple, elephantine trees. The air in the yard just in front of the house would be golden. In June, you could see the air, as if it were full of the faintest powder, flecked by droning bees dreamily gliding to and fro.

I opened my eyes to the cheap glitter of drunken, sweaty faces. How could I ever have let Doris convince me to leave? *It's not fair*, I thought to myself.

By the time Richard and Doris came back to the table, I'd worked myself up into such a state that

I stood up and said, 'It's time to leave,' and then walked out so they had to follow. I climbed into his car and sat behind the steering wheel, watching them stumble toward me, Doris clutching Richard's arm.

'I'll drive,' I said, and he got into the front seat beside me; he drunkenly felt around in his jeans pockets and handed over the keys. Doris touched him on the shoulder. 'Why don't you move over,' she said. 'Let's all ride up front.' He slid closer to me, and I could smell his whiskey, the stench of his pipe.

'I don't believe I've ever been this drunk,' Doris said as she slammed the door.

When we got back to Richard's house, I went straight up to bed, for I couldn't bear to watch it anymore. I heard commotion down in the living room—records playing, loud talk—but fell asleep all the same. I woke in the middle of the night, intending to go the bathroom, but didn't get farther than Doris's room. The door was open. I peered in and saw the bed was still made. A clock ticked solemnly on the dresser. It looked like a place someone had moved out of, so silent and bare. I padded across the floor to stand in the middle of the room, to accustom myself to its atmosphere. Then, out of old habit, I opened her closet to run my hands up and down the cool fabrics. I had just reached in, hadn't even touched anything, when I heard a hiss. I whipped around toward the door, but Doris wasn't there. It was just one of her new dresses falling off the hanger; it lay in a pile at my feet. I picked it up and held it against me, smoothing it across my body with one hand, as if to photograph myself into it with touch.

Chapter Four

THE NEXT MORNING, I woke up confused, thinking I was in my own bedroom. It took me a moment to remember that Doris had disappeared the night before, that, in fact, she had violated what I saw as our unspoken pact when it came to men. It wasn't the first time she'd been gone all night; but before she'd always tried to hide her absence, out of consideration to me and Dad. She used to slink into the house before he and I woke up—though I was always awake, waiting. No matter how early she came in, I was watching through a slit between my curtains as the car eased up the street, turned, bobbed on the hump of our driveway, and stopped. Then Doris slowly climbed out and turned to fish her overnight bag from the back seat.

This time, though, at Richard's, Doris had trapped me, so to speak—as if, now that Dad was gone, she wanted me to witness her philandering.

The more I thought about it, the more furious I became, so I decided not to get up—that's how I would show her just how angry I was. I dressed and lay down again on my bed. But, the truth was, I was afraid to go downstairs and face the two of them. If I couldn't pretend my sister's innocence, how would I behave? Wouldn't every one of my comments seem to allude to what had happened in Richard's bedroom last night?

I lay there perhaps an hour before I heard Doris and Richard talking in the kitchen, the clatter of dishes, water in the sink. A bit later, Doris came pounding up the stairs; I could tell just from that sound how elated she was.

She leaned into the doorway, breathless, and said, 'Hey, Frannie.' She was wearing the same black dress from yesterday and a cigarette was smoking in her hand. 'Want some breakfast?'

'I'm not hungry.'

'Yes you are. Come on. We're making eggs,' she said, keeping up that air of forced cheer.

'I know when I'm hungry, and I'm not—so go on and leave me alone.'

'Oh, quit this!' she said, taking a drag. 'For heaven's sake, you're acting like you're ten.'

I whispered so Richard wouldn't hear, 'And how do you expect me to act? What happened last night, Doris?' The frankness of my question, the anger in my voice, scared me.

'Well now,' she said, waving her cigarette giddily, 'we just got a little carried away. Just a little.' She pinched her thumb and finger together, to show a little.

I rubbed my face with my hands. 'Oh, Doris—why?'

'What do you mean "why"?' She came into the room and draped herself against the white wall, looking as prettily disheveled as a woman in an ad. I think in her mind, at that moment, she was larger than life, Marilyn Monroe or Jane Russell. How could I talk to this woman, this shifting apparition of hard eyes and cigarette smoke?

'I mean why, that's all,' I said. 'You barely know him, Doris. He has a girlfriend, maybe a lot of girlfriends.' I was strangely aware of the sound of my voice—it seemed like someone else's. I hadn't thought I'd be able to confront her like this.

'You don't understand,' she said, flopping down in the chair opposite me. 'That's the whole point. I'm just enjoying being with him. It's just a fling. Don't you see the appeal of that?'

'No. I think it's wrong.'

'Oh, for heaven's sake!' she said, 'I'm thirty-five. I've had a diaphragm for, what, nine years? Surely that doesn't come as a shock to you.'

Even a week earlier I might have continued to fuss, but something had changed—I'd began to understand that I couldn't bully Doris anymore, not the way I used to. 'I'm not shocked exactly,' I said calmly. 'But you know it shocks some people. Don't you think people talked behind your back all those years? And I always stuck up for you. I even lied to Dad for you—told him you were at girlfriends' houses—and you never once thanked me.'

She looked off a moment, absorbing this, and then said, 'I didn't ask you to lie for me, did I?'

'No.' Some new understanding of her sent pinpricks up my back.

'Well, maybe it would have been better if you hadn't helped me hide anything,' she said.

'And then what would have happened? Everything would have fallen apart.'

'Oh, Frannie,' she said, sounding tired. 'Everything *had* fallen apart. We just pretended it hadn't.'

'Don't blame me,' I said. 'You had something to hide, and you hid it.'

'I know, I know—I do regret that. I regret all the time I wasted doing what was easiest.' For a moment I was afraid she was going to cry, but then a hard look came over her face. 'Anyway, it doesn't matter now.'

'I suppose not,' I said. I didn't understand my own calm. For how many years had I feared exactly this confrontation, imagining myself stiff with wrath, cold with anger? What I never expected was my own acceptance of Doris's ways. 'Look,' I said, 'I wish you wouldn't do these things, but I can't stop you. I suppose I faced that long ago.'

Doris seemed not to hear me. 'I have to tell you something,' she said, with an odd flatness to her voice. 'You know, I never planned to stay at Aunt Katherine's. I was just humoring you.'

'You were?'

'Now don't get upset,' she said, holding her hand out as if she were about to touch me. 'Let me explain. I thought I'd go down there with you, and you'd get settled in, and eventually I could go off and make my own life. But then, when I talked about leaving, you wanted to go too. I don't think you could bear to spend the rest of your life in that house either.'

'I still plan to live there,' I protested. 'I admit, I did think it would be fun to go on a vacation. That's all it is, a vacation.' But already I was weakening. Already I was entertaining the possibility that I would not go back to Aunt Katherine's if that was what Doris wanted.

'I knew you couldn't wait to get on the road,' she said, jutting her chin out the way she always did. 'Because when we were leaving I saw you turn into another Frannie for a moment. I think that other Frannie is very tired of being a good little girl. You keep her hidden away, locked up, so she can't get into any trouble.'

I felt my forehead wrinkle. 'I don't think that's true. I don't see what you could possibly mean.'

'Trust me,' she said, taking another drag. 'I would have given up on you if it weren't true.'

A little thrill went through me at this idea— that I had a hidden wild side—though I suspected Doris had made this up, was only flattering me to get her way.

'Oh, I can't think about this anymore,' I said. 'Let's have some coffee.' And so we went downstairs, and Richard made us breakfast, ministering to us as if we were *both* his lovers, buttering my toast before he passed it to me.

Suddenly, I felt tremendously fond of the two of them. Oh miracle, my jealous heart melted.

*

OFTEN I FELT left out, but I tried to be pleasant; I even made dinner for them the next night while they went on a walk. Without speaking of it at all, Doris and I had reached an understanding. We would leave before Mim returned, and we would not, for the present, go back to Aunt Katherine's. Instead, we'd keep on driving.

So complete was our understanding that I was not surprised when, after dinner two nights later, Doris said, 'Well, we should be packing up, shouldn't we, Frannie? Got to get an early start tomorrow.' She was not usually one for early starts. I brightened, wiping my mouth carefully with a napkin to hide my pleased look.

'Yes, I suppose so.'

Richard's eyes darted from Doris to me, and I felt a rush of happiness. He seemed suddenly aware of the communication that ran between us like an undertow, a deep sweeping force. Now *he* was the one left out.

'I'm going to miss both of you. I wish you would stay for the summer.'

'You know I can't,' Doris looked up at him through her lashes.

'Yes,' he said, and paused. 'You'll come back though, won't you?'

'Of course,' Doris laid her hand on his. He cleared his throat, looked uncomfortable. 'You know, Mim sort of floats around. She's almost not there some-times. But with you,' he looked at Doris, and then quickly caught my eye, 'I don't know, with you two I feel like I'm rooted down in something. Cared for. Well, whatever,' he smiled at us now. 'Don't mind me.'

51

'Of course we'll mind you,' Doris said and kissed him on the cheek as she cleared his plate.

A FEW HOURS after we left, it began to rain. The windshield seemed to be melting where the wipers didn't reach. The road outside turned to a mist of hissing water. With the windows rolled up, the car became close and cozy. 'Aren't you sad, leaving him?' I asked.

She leaned over and fiddled with the radio, and I got a whiff of her stale-cigarette smell. All she could tune in was static, which she left on. 'Thank you for being so sweet, Frannie. I know you don't approve.'

'It's not that I don't approve—I don't *understand*,' I said. 'Why do you want to go to the trouble of getting so close to someone when you're never going to see him again? I've never understood that about you.'

She smiled over at me. 'Fran, all I want is for a man to look at me like I'm the most beautiful thing he's ever seen.'

'I know you do,' I said stiffly, 'but don't you think there's more to life than that?'

Doris breathed slowly, like someone asleep, as she drove. Finally she said, 'I guess in my heart I've never stopped being the popular girl at the high school prom. That's a damn pitiful thing, isn't it? Anyway I wasn't going to stay around and make things hard for him when Mim came back. It was time to go.'

She fell silent, absorbed in navigating the puddly, winding road. She had her hair back in a ponytail, which made her look girlish. I admired her then, her strong heart. But when she glanced at me again, she was wincing, her eyes squinted up as if she were about to cry. She said, 'Sometimes I'd swear there's something wrong with me. When I'm with a man, I feel like I'm watching a movie of myself. It's awful. That's why I could never stay with any of them. That's why, that horrible feeling of not being inside myself.'

'Whatever do you mean?' I glanced over at her, surprised at this intimation of weakness.

'I like them well enough for a while, but then, I don't know, something happens. I start pretending to be someone I'm not; I get so caught up in trying to act like a sort of lighthearted person that I don't realize what I'm doing. Suddenly, I turn into an awful stranger. Sometimes I can tell I'm contorting my face into whatever expression I believe he—the man—wants. And then I think "My God, how did this happen?"'

'You didn't feel that with Richard.' I said.

'No. But I still wanted to get away from him all the same. I never could stay with any of them. How was I ever supposed to get married?'

'Oh Doris,' I said. 'Lots of people don't marry. It's a great tradition in our family.'

'But at least you were in love,' she looked sideways at me accusingly. 'I didn't want to bring it up, but that's the way it is. At least you could.'

Peter was the head of a library in a town not far from ours, and for a time he was a fixture at our house—he ate dinner with us, played chess with Dad, fixed the wiring in the hallway and carried bags of

53

groceries up the front stairs. At night, after Dad was settled into bed and Doris had gone out, Peter would read to me—from Shakespeare or Dickens, I didn't care—and I would lie against him, my ear on his chest, listening to the way the words were inside him. The sound was like the rumble of cars far away. And I loved to have my cheek against his sweater; it smelled of him, the warm air that had been near his body, and of wool coats, and of old books.

I didn't feel the grand passion for him described in some of the books he read to me; rather, it was as if something I hadn't understood before had become clear. They say I glowed then, that I became suddenly beautiful.

He never did propose. After a year or so, I saw how his mind was wandering when he was with me, as if he had come to a tiresome passage in a book. And after two years, he got himself engaged to the kind of woman who always knew what to say at a party.

Even at the height of his love for me, when he came over every night, when sometimes he would forget what he was saying and just stare at me, I'd known it couldn't last. So when he took me to dinner to tell me he'd fallen in love with Eva, I told him, 'I know.'

Peter had leaned forward; his glasses caught the light, making his eyes seem to go blank. 'You could hate me a little.'

But the truth was, I'd always understood longing better than love—and I loved Peter now in memory more than I ever did in life. Often, little scenes would come back to me, surprising in their vividness: the way he held my hand under a lamp to see how badly I'd been cut, or the way he did dishes at our sink, the sleeves of his stiff white shirt rolled up and his tie hanging over one shoulder so it wouldn't get wet. I remember, too, his horn-rimmed glasses on our coffee table.

Doris said, 'I saw how you were. I've never been like that. So don't resent me for trying as best as I can.'

We drove for a long time without saying anything. I was thinking of Peter—only a few months ago, I'd run into him in the drugstore. He'd fixed me with a long, steady gaze. 'Frannie,' he said, 'I was just thinking about you. How are you?'

'I am all right,' I said flatly. 'How's Eva?' I shot that question back like an insult, a curse on his fickle heart.

'Oh, she's all right, I suppose.' Peter looked lost then; I could tell the conversation wasn't going at all the way he meant it to.

'Well, good to see you,' I called, darting out of the store so quickly that I forgot to pick up Dad's pills.

That exchange with Peter, it left me terribly upset. He had wanted something from me—absolution probably—and for days my heart beat fast whenever the phone rang. I was certain that he'd call and ask me to a dinner at his house, with Eva. Well, I would just plain refuse to come. Why should I sit at his table and chitchat, pretend we were friends and there were no hard feelings? Just thinking about it made me fume. But I never did hear from him again.

*

FOR A LONG time, I gazed out my window, which was so steamed up from the rain that the passing trees looked like a forest in a fairy tale. When Doris rolled down the window to throw out a cigarette butt, the water under our tires sounded as loud and crazy as applause.

After some time, she pulled up in front of a roadside store, a shack with a Coca-Cola sign over it. Inside, the rain on the tin roof was a constant dull roar, and the little aisles were packed with canned milk, Wonderbread, marshmallows, peanut butter. Doris brought a pack of cigarettes and a candy bar to the man at the counter. His stomach spilled over his belt buckle and his big damp hands could barely make change.

He looked at Doris and said, 'I feel terrible depressed too, sister. It's the rain.' His eyes darted from one of us to the other, and I think we both felt what it must be like to be in the store alone all day, to be carrying so much fat with never a rest from it, ever.

All of a sudden, Doris seemed to sag. Outside, we stood on the little porch beside the ice machine, and she handed me the keys. 'You drive.'

When we got in the car, she slumped against the door, watching the raindrops making their slow way down the window.

'Where do you want to go?'

'I don't care . . . I don't even want to know.'

I didn't start the car; instead, I looked out at the rain turning the ground to yellow mud, peeling the white paint from the store, gathering in murky puddles everywhere.

'There's something else,' she said. 'Richard and I talked a lot—that is, I talked a lot—and somehow it started me thinking. What I don't understand is why I stayed in that house, moldering away. Think of it—in a few years I'm going to be forty. And I wasted my youth just waiting for something to happen. I was so afraid of getting trapped, of losing my freedom, that I didn't see how I'd already lost it. I should have just up and left. But then Dad got sick, and . . . I don't know.' Her voice began to quaver. 'Richard says it's a sad story, and I agree.' Then she began crying in a way that frightened me—openly, unashamedly. She gasped for breath, shutting her eyes, but remained slumped in her seat. She didn't even lift her hands to her face.

'You're just all worked up after this business with Richard. You'll feel better in a day or two.'

She tried to say something but was crying too hard.

I started the engine—and, making an effort to sound cheerful, said, 'Well, I would say we might as well see our country and have some fun. This will be our vacation, and then maybe you'll want to go back to Aunt Katherine's.'

Doris shook her head, crying, and I vowed never to say anything so brutally stupid again.

THAT NIGHT, SOON after we passed a sign that welcomed us to Asheville, North Carolina, I found a motel and went to register, leaving Doris in the car. When I came back from the office, she hadn't budged from her seat. She sat smoking, looking out at the highway with her head tilted, as if she were listening to the occasional roar of a truck and the country sound of crickets.

'Doris,' I said, 'we have a room. Come on, get your bag.' She climbed out and bent over the back of the car. The light from the motel's neon sign lit up her bare arms and face a purplish pink. She was beautiful in her misery then, my sister. In the room, she leaned against the wall, looking out the window at the highway, the headlights sweeping past. She touched the window pane. 'There's nothing lonelier than the highway—after a while, you don't even have yourself anymore.'

I knew what she meant. With each motel, each diner, I felt more anonymous, wiped clean.

'I like it,' she said. 'It makes me feel better.' And then she looked at me, 'I'm so glad you're with me, Frannie, because I just feel so confused.'

I met her eyes, my face composed, and said, 'I wish I could do more for you.' But when I turned away, I was smiling to myself. I was sitting on one of the beds, examining the key that was attached to a plastic oval with our room number on it. Right then, I was washed over by happiness at knowing that she needed me, and this wonderful feeling somehow was connected with the key. I clutched the bright little key, and the bite of its sharp edges into my skin filled me with joy, and when I opened my hand again I saw it had etched its shape on my palm.

Chapter Five

THE NEXT DAY, I drove us through the
Smoky Mountains. Every so often, the car would
plunge into tight tunnels of trees and out into flashes
of sunlight. Somewhere along the highway in Tennessee, we came to a place for honeymooners. There were
several motels—one of them, meant to look Spanish,
was stacked up high in the air like a wedding cake. Its
sign read, JUST MARRIED? WE'VE GOT SPECIAL DISCOUNTS.
In between the motels were tin-roofed souvenir shacks
with ceramic black bears posed in lines out front; down
the highway I glimpsed the spidery towers of an
amusement park. When we drove past it, I could hear
the thunder of the rollercoaster and the screams of its
riders. I imagined the rollercoaster packed with newly-
weds clutching each other as they plunged down the
twisting threads of track. The violent rattling of the
wheels would make their bodies vibrate and their teeth
chatter, but to them the fear would feel delicious.

It got me thinking how love and terror aren't so far apart, really. Since I'd taken over the driving, Doris had mostly fallen silent, so I talked without expecting an answer from her. Now I said, 'You know what I think? Maybe you haven't missed anything by not falling in love—because falling in love isn't so different from just plain falling apart.' I was thinking of Peter, the first time I saw him sitting behind his library desk with his legs crossed tight, the way a woman does. It was only a few weeks after we'd found out about Dad. The doctors had said he'd linger on for years, that eventually he wouldn't be able to speak or move for himself. There was always a sour feel in my stomach then, knowing what was ahead for all of us. But when I saw Peter, I forgot all of that—or maybe I should say it changed into something I could live with, a fluttery, terrified infatuation.

60

I positioned myself down an aisle of books and watched him as he hunched over something on his desk. He had a habit of swallowing hard, so his Adam's apple bobbed. When he rubbed his cheek, I could hear the faint hiss of his hand against stubble. I smelled him too, or imagined I did, a perfume of something sweet, like graham crackers, and also musky, something like the refined leather of old volumes of Ovid or Defoe. I grabbed the first convenient book, by Robert Frost, hurried to his desk and asked to check it out. When he looked up at me I felt a stab—not, as they always say, in the heart, but in my stomach, as if I had a bad case of gas. He held the book, seeming to weigh it, and asked, 'What is your opinion of Frost?' And that's how we got talking and went out to lunch and all the rest of it, while my father struggled just to sit up in that darkened room.

I THOUGHT WHAT Doris needed was something to take her out of herself. She had been hunched gloomily in the passenger seat, sometimes smoking down a cigarette, since we'd left in the morning. I pulled into the parking lot of a restaurant made of simulated stone, with a fake-looking wooden mill wheel turning in the river beside it. Even the river, which was unquestionably real, looked fake.

'Come on,' I said. 'It's one of those pancake houses where they put whipped cream and sprinkles on.'

'Good,' she said, seeming to come awake as she climbed out of the car. 'I love god-awful places like this.'

'I know.' It was one of the weaknesses we shared.

As soon as we sat down inside and got our coffee, Doris perked up. 'Whatever's wrong in my life,' she said, between sips, 'at least I don't have to wear a polyester waitress outfit.'

I felt a burst of pride then, that I'd roused her out of her funk. Ever since that moment standing in the rain, when she'd handed me the car keys, things had been different. I was taking care of her. More than that, something in her—and thus our lives—had shifted; from now on, I thought, she would confide in me as she never had before. I would finally gain a grip on that slippery soul.

Perhaps that was why I agreed to wear the

61

dress. We'd just finished eating and I began complaining about how dirty my clothes were, how I could feel the grime on my collar.

And Doris had said—as if it meant nothing, as if she were just throwing out the idea—'Well then, why don't you borrow one of my dresses.' I don't think she'd ever offered to lend me any of her clothing before.

'Do you mean it?' I said.

'Sure. You could try on that green one. I haven't even worn it. It's still in the tissue.'

'Oh, really, I couldn't do that,' I objected, without much conviction.

Of course, in the end I'd give in. I always used to beg to wear her clothes when we were teenagers, but she'd never let me—'You copy me enough as it is,' she'd say. And so I'd tried on her skirts and sweaters in secret, up in our room when she was gone. I loved to put on her things, to smell their faint traces of Doris, to feel the fabric sliding across my skin as it slid across hers. Like the other girls in school, Doris wore tight sweaters to show off her plump breasts and the cruel cut of her waist. Those same sweaters made me look as ugly as some kind of insect—long, bony arms and a sexless torso. So in that locked room I'd stuff my bra with cotton balls, put on a tight belt, rouge my cheeks, and then gaze at myself in the mirror. In those moments, I imagined that I had become her.

Now, a dangerous idea entered my head: *Maybe I could be beautiful after all*. 'It'd be interesting, just to see how the dress fits,' I said.

'That's right. All you have to do is try it on

in the bathroom here, so I can see how it looks on you. You pay our check; I'll go get the dress.' Before I could say anything, she was gone.

A few minutes later, I found myself in a locked bathroom stall, sliding out of my dark blue gaberdine dress and hanging it carefully on the door. Standing in nothing but my underwear and stockings, next to a toilet that was hissing because it wouldn't flush properly, I suddenly doubted the whole endeavor.

'Doris,' I called out. 'This is ridiculous.'

'Oh come on, let's just see!'

I slid the dress over my shoulders, and it fell over my body with a whisper. I opened the door.

'Here, give me your clothes,' Doris said. 'Don't hunch over like that. Now let's see.' She pushed me toward the full-length mirror.

63

For a moment, I couldn't bear how I looked. The dress—a sleeveless shift with a full skirt— showed my knuckled knees, the deep hollows of my armpits, the flatness of my chest. 'It's awful,' I said, close to tears.

'Oh, don't give me that,' she said. 'I wish I looked as good. You could be a model, I swear. You look exquisite—even though it hangs kind of low.'

'I'm too skinny,' I said. But slowly my vision was adjusting, the way you get used to sunlight when you walk outside. Then I began to see that I *did* look good: there was an Audrey Hepburn elegance to my long white arms and my bare neck. I turned, letting the skirt swing, studying myself. I felt almost naked with the air on my shoulders, my legs free. 'It doesn't feel right,' I said.

'You'd look great with a little make-up,' she said.

'Now, don't you push your luck.'

'Well,' she said, 'will you at least leave the bathroom? Can we at least get in the car?'

As we walked through the restaurant, I was almost surprised that no one glanced up at me. No, the families were bent over their meals, too involved in their own dramas to notice the woman in the new summer dress. Still, I felt as if I was parading around in some kind of crazy costume.

It put me in mind of that Halloween party Doris threw one year in high school. Our Cousin Bobby—he was always strange—showed up dressed as Lana Turner. Sometimes for talent shows, the boys in our school would imitate women, but it only made them seem more masculine, the cleavage of their dresses showing off the muscles on their necks and shoulders. Not Bobby. Every hair of his platinum wig was in place and he smoked a pretend cigarette with cool grace of a star. He carried it off like a boy who had practiced too many times in front of the mirror.

I'd felt an odd sympathy for him that day. After all, how many times had my fingers snuck across the fabrics in Doris's closet? How many times had I hastily stripped off my own clothes, slipped one of her dresses over my head, and felt it fall into place like a new personality? I knew what it was to lock the door and stand in front of the mirror in the stuffy closeness of an upstairs bedroom, where the sun coming through the curtain crack makes you feel sick because it reminds you of bare trees and frost-burnt meadows and glinting cars, ordinary things belonging to decent people.

At those times, I thought I'd never learn to be an ordinary or decent person. I was thirteen, and this was only one of many private rituals I performed in the nauseating closeness of a shut-up room.

'WHY DON'T YOU buy some new clothes when we get to Nashville?' Doris asked. I didn't argue. I was driving, still wearing her dress, its skirt crumpled all around my legs on the car seat. I should have changed back into my own clothes, but I hadn't.

'Look. Isn't it lovely?' I said. We were whizzing through the lush, hilly country of Tennessee. The sky was the blue of morning glories, a color made all the more dramatic by the green tint of the windshield. Beside us on the highway, a hippie couple drove a broken-down van; long strands of the woman's hair waved like streamers in the wind. There hadn't been any hippies to speak of in New Hampshire—I mean real ones. Ever since we'd started driving, though, I'd been catching glimpses of them camping at rest stops or walking by the side of the road.

Doris lay back against her seat with the satisfied sigh of someone who'd had several cups of coffee and a plate of pancakes. 'I don't know why in the world I've been moping, Fran. We have money. We're young—or at least we're not as old as we could be. Do you realize how lucky we are? We can do *anything* we want.'

'But after Memphis, what then?' I said. We had already decided to visit our cousins there, had called Aunt Katherine to have her send some of our things on ahead of us.

'Look at them,' she said, gazing at the hippie van. 'Where do you suppose they're headed?'

'California. That's what you hear on the news. They all go out to California.'

'Hmmm,' Doris said. 'I heard they drive around searching for America. I don't know what that means, but I read it somewhere.'

'Aren't we searching for America, too?' I asked. I had one arm out the window, resting on the side of the car, and suddenly was aware of the terrible force of that wind on my skin. This idea—that America, so familiar, was the crux of a great mystery—filled me with the same sort of exhilaration as that crushing, crazy air.

'We're searching for something, that's for sure, because we're just a couple of small-town girls. We don't know anything about life.'

'Of course we do,' I said. 'Don't you think there's as much life in New Hampshire as anywhere else?'

'I suppose.' She snapped on the radio to listen to the news. The announcer was giving that day's body count from Vietnam. 'How terrible,' she said, turning up the volume.

I hated to think about the war, so wrong and stupid, so unstoppable. I said, 'What about our war, Doris? Can you remember it?'

And then we just naturally lapsed into our old way of talking—about the past rather than the future, each of us dredging up details to make it seem more vivid.

'That was a very strange time, the war,' Doris said. 'It should have been the worst time in my life, but I believe I was happy through most of it.'

'Yes, that's how I feel,' I said. 'Having Mom all to ourselves. No rules. But you know, there was also a lot of misery then, too—the way we were made fun of in school and all the horrible things they said about Dad.'

Mother had told us not to breathe a word to the other children about our father. Of course, she said, if they asked us straight out, we mustn't lie. But we should say that he was serving, just as bravely, here in America. We were supposed to tell them about the sea water.

We first heard about it in one of his letters. My mother always read these with great ceremony after dinner. 'Let's clear all the dishes first,' she'd say. Doris and I would carefully take the plates into the kitchen. 'And let's wash them, too,' she'd add, still in her apron, the letter held in one hand, the hand with her wedding ring. Doris washed and I dried, both of us working slowly. We all wanted to put it off, the letter reading, because there was no time bleaker than afterward, when we'd have to start waiting all over again for another letter.

When we were finished with the dishes, my mother would take off her faded flowery apron and hang it on a peg. Then the three of us would troop into the living room. Mom would unfold the letter, settle down in her chair, clear her throat, and begin.

Doris and I never quite understood the letters. They were written to our mother about the worries and delights of the adult world—money,

67

furloughs, the sadness of bright men shunned by their country. But we loved hearing his words, and the way our mother's voice became scratchy with tenderness as she read. After the letter, she explained what our father had said as if it were a bedtime story. And in the first month or so, it seemed as exciting as a book or movie. 'Your father's staying in a camp in the woods. He lives in a cabin. He's working very hard to clear out a swamp so that someday people can live in it.'

But though we thought it sounded lovely, there was something about our father's lot that made Mom angry. She used shake her head and cluck, 'Girls, it's a shame. They could use his wonderful brains, but they've made him a ditch digger.' Then, sometimes, she'd add, 'And he thought he'd be helping poor people.' I never understood why she said he was clearing out a swamp but called him a ditch digger, as if she didn't care to get straight what job our father had.

Once I asked, 'If he's digging ditches, isn't that helping people in a way?'

'I suppose. But it's a terrible waste of our educated people, don't you see?' she said, and then went on with her argument as if I were an adult, so that I understood not a word.

Several months after he'd been gone, Mom got a letter she wouldn't read us. We sat down in the living room anyway, and she explained it to us. 'Your Daddy feels that he hasn't been doing important work—hasn't been able to bring food to the poor people up in the mountains, like he wanted to—and so he's chosen to do a very brave thing,' she said. Then she was silent a minute.

'He's volunteered to be in an experiment. Remember the story I read you once about the shipwrecked sailors who don't dare drink from the sea because it would make them sick?' Doris and I nodded, although I don't believe we'd ever heard such a story.

'That's what can happen to people in boats that are bombed,' she said, 'and that's why the scientists are going to have your father drink sea water.'

The way she'd explained it, I pictured him draining down one glass of salty water, and that would be that. But there wasn't another letter for a long time. Finally, when one did come it wasn't from our father, but a doctor. Dad was delirious, and they were putting him back on fresh water again. A few weeks later, we heard from my father himself. He was better, but they were still giving him salt water, now mixed with fresh.

In short, my father lived on sea water and emergency rations for almost a year. Later, he told us that when they brought him his water he often gagged it all up again; he always felt thirsty, couldn't stop licking his lips, but would taste only the dreadful salt. When he didn't have a fever, they put him back to work in the swamp, because it helped to 'simulate the exertions of a shipwrecked man.' He worked slowly with his shovel, trying not to sweat.

That's how the government was with the C.O.s: it saw them as stubborn men who needed to be punished. Of course, Doris and I understood none of that. All we knew was that our father chose to drink sea water rather than go to war, which seemed

69

to us a fair trade. But it was impossible to explain this to the children at school.

My mother, with a typical hazy lack of judgment, had assumed that they would be too polite to ask about our father. But no such etiquette was observed. With their hands on their hips and their feet splayed, they'd say, 'Where's your Dad? He's not at war, is he?'

My father's sea-water drinking, which had sounded so heroic when my mother told it, seemed like a rotten excuse, and so I betrayed him. I'd say, 'My father *is too* fighting.'

It didn't matter how I lied. They could see my dresses were homemade, my shoes were coming apart at the seams, and my lunch was mostly bread in the same paper bag as yesterday's. In the years before the war, our family had been one of the richest in town. Doris and I had worn fancy crinoline dresses that were the envy of the other girls. We'd been as smug as rich children can be, reciting our Christmas gifts to classmates who'd gotten nothing.

But the other children's fathers were now sending home war wages, riches that most families had never known during the Depression. While we grew thin and our clothes worn, they grew plump-faced and cheerful; and, despite the rations, some brought meat and cake for lunch.

Doris and I, in the matching dresses our mother had made, walked close together everywhere, our own little battalion, ready to fend off the kicks and the jeers. It was the year we made up our own language. Doris was greatly impressed by the idea that every country had its own secret code. The Japs had one, and so did the Germans and the Americans. Though we never understood the intricacies of why such codes were used, we knew one thing: language was a tool of war. And so Doris and I spoke to one another in a babble. I'm still not certain whether or not we understood one another; though it seemed at the time we interpreted each others' strange patois and frantic hand motions with ease, when I think back on it, it seems impossible. How could two small children invent and remember an entire language?

Far worse than the scorn of children was the pity of adults. My teacher sometimes brought an extra bottle of milk for me; when she thought none of the other children were watching, she'd kneel down beside me at my desk, where I ate lunch, and say, 'I can't drink all of my milk, how would you like some, Frannie?'

71

I'd play along with her, though my eyes were threatening to brim with tears, as if I'd just been scolded. 'Why, thank you,' I'd say. 'I am rather thirsty.' After she left my desk, I'd drink it in gulps, thinking guiltily of my father choking on his sea water.

When Dad did come home, gaunt and changed, there was no time for him to rest. The savings were gone; his old supply company had been boarded up for years. He took me there, once, to look the place over. I remember how he stuck the key into the padlock, his hand weak, and set his shoulder to the door to ram it open. When we were inside, I leaned against the wall, feeling the cold of the cement floor through my shoes. Dad walked up to a bale of hay, took a handful, and sniffed it. 'Trash,' he said.

He wandered over to a pile of machinery, disturbing some pigeons who'd roosted there. They swooped up to the rafters, banging against the beams. The batter of their wings—the way they couldn't just land somewhere but had to keep flying up, startled—scared me. Dad stooped on the other side of the warehouse, turning a piece of metal over and over in his hands, as if it were a key and he were trying to figure out what door it went to.

It wasn't long before he recovered enough to get the business going again—my father always had a gift for predicting trends, for making the right investment. 'The war has changed the technology of farming forever,' he'd say, and he found several business partners to put up money so he could stock the warehouse with sheet plastic, nylon nozzles, prefabricated sheds you could put together with just a few nails—things no one had ever seen in our town before.

Still, in another way, my father's recovery was only superficial. A certain moral light in him had died. Two pieces of information, two terrible facts about the war, had fallen on him like the atomic bombs that destroyed Japan.

He told me once that, before the war, he had believed along with the other clever young men of socialist leanings that the news of the Nazi atrocities was all propaganda. Such rumors—of Germans making lampshades out of human skin, for example—were similar to lies that had circulated before the earlier world war.

After he came home, though, he found that he and the bright young men had been wrong about the Nazis. My father couldn't forgive himself for that. 'I was so full of myself,' he said to me a long time later. 'I thought the worst the world could offer in the way of evil was some hill people starving in backwoods Kentucky, so I decided to go save them and turn my back on the war. I never figured that all the atrocity stories could be true, that I was ducking out of the real fight.' Perhaps he hadn't gained a new understanding of evil so much as he'd finally come to recognize the evil that sat even in the silent meeting hall of his good Quaker heart.

And that year, another piece of devastating news came to him. A friend of his from the C.O. camps sent him a clipping from a medical journal: it turned out that the Navy, doing its own testing, had found a way to treat sea water so that it could be drunk safely. There had been no need for his yearlong ordeal, all his delirium and shakes and hallucinations.

73

I believe now that it was not the sea water but these two bits of news that so changed our father. Something about him became vulnerable, caved in, crushed. Long before Mom died, long before Dad himself began to die, he lost his faith. And it was then—when I was still a little girl—that I began to take care of him.

WE DIDN'T TRUST Nashville. It had the hard look of a big city and the atmosphere of a county fair where you know all the games are loaded and the freaks are fake. Men walked around in polyester, pearl-snap cowboy shirts, and if you looked at them too long they'd ask for a handout.

But I found a store I liked, a place with

creaking wood floors, a slow ceiling fan, and simple clothes. I bought above-the-knee skirts, cotton tops, sandals. 'I look like I'm about to play tennis,' I told Doris when I stood before her in one of the outfits, 'but I don't care.' She urged me to buy other things, too—a black linen dress and a pair of silk slacks.

That night, we checked into a fancy hotel downtown and went out for a movie, like girls on a lark. As we walked the few blocks back to our hotel, each holding an ice cream cone, she said, 'Now this isn't so bad, is it?'

'Not at all. In fact, I'm having a wonderful, wonderful time,' I said, turning my head fast to look around so the neon lights of the bars and clubs would turn to streaks across my eyes. 'It's going to be hard to go back to real life.' She just laughed like she knew something I didn't.

THE NEXT DAY, Sunday, we drove to Memphis, which seemed like a ghost town after Nashville. Newspaper pages glided across the wide sidewalks; stoplights swung and bounced on their wires in the hot wind, signaling to empty streets. The deserted downtown had the atmosphere of a house that's been shut up and abandoned for the summer.

We looked for signs of the riots we'd heard so much about, but only saw some boarded-up windows. I can never think of that tragedy—the strike that Dr. King had tried to lead, which had gone violent like everything else during that violent year—without thinking of my father dying.

We'd brought him to the hospital when his pain pills stopped working, and he'd become so thin that his pale hazel eyes seemed to have grown to the size of pennies. We borrowed a wheelchair from the hospital, a gleaming horrible thing, and I remember kneeling on the living room floor to lift each of his slippered feet onto a metal flap. He'd tried to say something, and I leaned toward him. 'What is it, Dad?'

'Now this is the life,' he whispered—talking was hard for him. 'I feel like a Chinese dowager.'

I turned so he couldn't see my face. He was joking, though he knew that after we wheeled him out, he would never see the house again; never again the blue couch where he'd sat with our mother; never again the stand-up lamp and the braided rug.

As I took him outside, I was crying, but he couldn't see. On the front walk he held up one hand. Doris had the Valiant waiting, its back door yawning open for him.

'Stop Frannie, stop,' he whispered. 'Look how beautifully you've kept the yard.' And I did look—at the tender grass just coming up in the gingerbread-colored earth and the mossy branches of the elm trees and the sky like the thinnest blue glass. I saw with his eyes, and all of it seemed fragile and dear, shimmering with meaning; the tremor of the leaves seemed a shiver of pleasure. To this day, I can see the world that way if I want to—living and dying, mesh of joy and pain, perishable and indestructable. But I try to avoid thinking like that. A person could go crazy that way.

A few hours later, I sat beside Dad in his hospital bed with the metal bars. He couldn't talk because of the tubes they had in him, but I knew

75

what he wanted, and when seven o'clock came, I snapped on the TV for the news. Dad read, or had read to him, every paper and watched every news program—I think he half-believed that as long he kept up with current events, he'd remain alive. In the past year, because of reading to Dad, I felt like I could name all the battles of Vietnam—though I can't remember exactly what happened in those battles. Still, the Vietnam words have stuck in my head and become confused with the medical terms I learned because of Dad's illness: My Lai, Lotramine, Lon Nol, lymphoid, narceine, napalm.

That particular night, I remember, it wasn't the faint palm fronds of Vietnam on TV, but our own Memphis—a negro man explaining how he couldn't feed his family on what they paid him to collect garbage. My father's speckled hand tightened on my own. I knew what he would say if he could: 'I'd be there. Oh, Frannie, I may not have fought my war, but I'd be there if I could.' Less than a month later, Dr. King stood on the balcony of a motel in Memphis. He stood on the balcony and he took the air, and a bullet raked off one side of his face. It was a mighty death. It was the death I wished for my father. In the end, my father became a stranger to us, a husk of himself, a withered thing. I lost him little by little, like pieces of my own flesh being cut out. He died after he had already died. The sound of his death was not a gunshot, but the phone ringing early in the morning the day after Dr. King was killed.

When you turned on the TV back then, it was all funerals, linked arms and crumpled, crying faces. In my mind, it was my father they were mourning, not Dr. King. It was my father who gave the great speech about a promised land, who stood on that balcony and was shattered by a bullet at the very moment he was shimmering, he was shining with the light of the righteous.

I HADN'T SEEN Annie since we were both kids, and I remembered her as uncharacteristically cheerful, buxom, and pink-cheeked for our family. She ran off to marry Chuck when she was a teenager, which had made her always seem rather scandalous and impulsive to me, though she'd been settled for almost twenty years.

When we drove up to her house—a split-level out where the suburbs yielded to country—a brace of dogs surrounded our car, barking up a storm. A heavy woman with black glasses and a bouffant hairdo appeared in the doorway. 'Hey, Rocky, Winnie, leave them alone!' she belted out. As we emerged from the car, I minced away from the eager dogs and their muddy paws, frightened they would dirty my new skirt.

'Just give them a good shove if they bug you,' she called as we approached. At the door, she folded each of us into her embrace. She wore slacks and a t-shirt and smelled of hairspray. 'Oh, it is *so* good to see family!' she said, breathing out a sigh.

We both mumbled something polite.

'Well, that's grand,' she said. 'Come on in and put your feet up. I swear to God, Rocky—get *out* of here.' We followed her into the house. A tangle of raincoats lay by the door. The furniture was covered with dog hairs and the floor littered with magazines, ashtrays, and books.

'What a lovely house you have,' I stammered.

'Place is a mess,' she said. 'What with all the dogs and Peggy, I've given up.' She led us into the kitchen, cleared stacks of newspapers off some chairs, and poured us lemonade.

'Looking at you two,' she said, 'if I had to guess your ages, I'd say twenty-two and twenty-four. I should never have had kids. That's when I gained all this weight.'

Before either of us could come up with a polite response to this, the phone rang and one of the dogs began barking. '*Shush*,' she said. 'I'm tired of you.' With a practiced movement, she pushed the dog out the back door and grabbed the phone. 'Chuck? The hay people didn't come. That's right. OK, hold on.' She looked over her glasses at us, 'Aunt Kathy sent you some packages—they're upstairs. Your mail's right there, on the counter.'

Doris found the letters that Aunt Katherine had forwarded and began sorting them. After a minute, she stopped and carefully slid one envelope from the pile. 'Here's a letter for you, Fran,' she said, giving me a look. It was from Peter.

Chapter Six

'EXCUSE ME,' I said, and got up. I found
my way out of the house and opened the car door to
get in behind the wheel: the car was the only place
that felt private to me now.

The letter crackled in my hand, smelling of
him, or so I imagined. I opened it carefully and pulled
out two typewritten pages. It was hot in the car, and
I felt dizzy holding the blinding white sheets of paper
that not long ago had left our town, with its fat river
bristling with hairy reeds and its solemn houses so
dark and cool inside.

'Dearest Frannie,' the letter began. 'I was
very sorry to hear about your father. I meant to
call you, but was preoccupied with a tragedy of my
own.

My marriage is falling apart and I
believe we're headed for a divorce. Eva and I
were never right for one another, not even at the

start. It's hard to say why without sounding bitter, except that she's high-spirited, and you know how I am. The result is, we're miserable. But I imagine you don't want to hear about that.

I worked up my courage and wrote this letter because I had to tell you how important you are to me. I believe you're the only woman I've ever loved—this I understand only now that I've made a terrible mistake.

Don't take me wrong, Frannie, but I knew that as long as your father was alive you wouldn't have married me—or if you had, it wouldn't have been a real marriage. Remember what it was like whenever we spent the day together? I'd see you get that look that meant you couldn't hear a word I said, and sure enough, in a minute you'd say you had to call the house again. He was sick, and you wanted to be with him. I certainly don't blame you for that.

Then I met Eva, who doted on me. I suppose I loved being fussed over and paid attention to more than I loved her. And as you know, she can be very charming. But underneath her charm there is nothing like your wisdom or intelligence.

I've made a dreadful mistake, and I only hope that, even if you no longer love me, we can at least resume our deep sympathy as friends. I realize now that you're another part of me. Sometimes when I'm thinking, I find I am explaining my actions or ideas to someone. Invariably that person is you.

It has been very difficult to write this

letter. Please forgive me as I try to untangle my life.

       With deepest love,
       Peter.'

I turned over the pages, but there was no more. I'd been so absorbed in the letter that when I looked up it was as if the world, stopped like a broken movie, had started up again. Dogs were barking somewhere in the woods; the cicadas began buzzing again; the sun on the hood of the car was too bright to look at; and I noticed all of a sudden how I was sweating.

I opened the car door and put one foot on the ground. I sat like that for a minute, feeling the breeze, and then tucked the letter into my purse, and went inside.

I could hear the buzz of voices in the kitchen, and not wanting to face Doris or Annie yet, I ducked into a bathroom. It was decorated like the rest of the house, a pink toilet with a shag rug cover on its lid. I leaned against the wall and stared at myself in the mirror. Against Annie's silver, op-art wallpaper, I looked positively freakish: my mouth grim and my hair piled on my head to form a grotesque bulge.

And what was I inside? Did I really have the strength of character, the angelic soul, that Peter believed I did? Truth to tell, there wasn't any self inside me that I could call good or bad. Instead, I was nothing but a jumble of memories—the creak of screen doors and the smell of flannel nightshirts and candy wrappers fished from the cracks of movie

81

theater seats and the water in the sink turning my fingers fat and light green. I was nothing but a lot of lived moments piled together like odds and ends at a church tag sale.

I suppose I had always thought of myself as a forgotten item at a tag sale, something in the corner one barely notices—out-of-date, homely, but with its own nostalgic charm. Peter's letter changed that. Not all at once, of course, but as I stood in the stuffy bathroom, the words in the letter gradually worked on me like a stiff drink of whiskey.

Somebody loved me more than I loved him. It had never occurred to me before that this could happen. I had always been the one who pined for other people; I had turned myself into a shrine dedicated to Doris and Dad, and even Peter. I carried a jumble of memories in my head, memories of my dear ones, like the decaying relics that martyrs carry, bone in a jar and tooth wrapped in cloth.

I learned to love that way from my mother. She saved every one of my father's letters, laying each like a delicate petal into a special box. When he was home, she gazed at him greedily when he talked to her—as if she were memorizing every word. And he was busy, busy, busy—gone on business trips, working late, taking a walk, locked away in the basement. He had a private world, and she did not. This imbalance between them infected us, Doris and Mom and me, with a constant uneasiness. Would he call and say he'd be late? Would he come back at all? Who was he with and where? It makes me wince to remember how she could smoke down a pack of cigarettes, her hand resting on the heavy, black receiver of the phone, waiting.

Now Peter was the one with his hand on the phone, waiting for me.

I FOUND DORIS out on the back porch, drinking and gazing at the picturesque pasture land. 'Annie went off to do something or other,' she said. 'Here, have half of this.' She poured the rest of her beer into a glass and handed to me. 'That must be some letter, Fran. You just disappeared on us.'

'It certainly took me by surprise,' I said, sitting down and crossing my legs, which I kept bare now. I let one of my sandals flop off my foot onto the floor. 'Here,' I said, handing her the letter.

She read slowly, moving her lips now and again, as if trying to act out the lines to herself. Then she looked up, smiling. 'Well, Fran, I'm really not surprised. He always was crazy about you. So, tell me, what are going to do?'

'I don't know. He's still married, so really all I can do is be flattered.'

'Good, I'm glad to hear you talk that way. Some women wouldn't be able to keep their sense of perspective after a letter like that.' She cocked her head as she lit another menthol. 'Want one?' she said, holding out the pack.

'No, of course not,' I said. But I took the pack and turned it around in my hands, examining the cellophane wrap, the neat rows of cigarettes inside. 'Well, just this once,' I relented, sliding one out. 'Can't I light it without having to put it in my mouth? It's so dirty.'

83

'Honestly,' she chided, taking the cigarette from me and lighting it from the end of hers.

She handed it back, and I tried to perch it between my fingers the way she did. 'I don't want to smoke it—just to hold it,' I said. 'I want to hold it while I tell you this, so I'll feel like someone else.'

'Who?'

'Oh, you know,' I said, 'the kind of woman who's familiar with this sort of situation. Like you.'

'Me?' she laughed. '*Me?* I've never gotten a letter like that.'

I flicked the ashes into the beer bottle top as I'd seen her do. 'Doris,' I said. 'Peter's wrong in that letter. He thinks I wouldn't have married him because I was too worried about Dad. The truth is, Peter drifted away from me, and I didn't know how to bring him back. Even so, I kept assuming we'd be together the rest of our lives. Then one day I looked over at him—he was driving me somewhere—and I thought *That man isn't going to marry me.* It was one of those things you realize just like that, like a clap of thunder. And you know how I could tell? It was just the way he sat behind the wheel, so self-important, squinting ahead at the road in the dark, all that concentration. He was suddenly acting as if driving was this terribly difficult thing, but I knew the truth was, he just didn't want to have to talk to me. I could see by the way he drove that he didn't love me.'

She considered this a moment. 'What if you were wrong?'

'What do you mean *wrong*? Why would he have married Eva if I was wrong?'

'Oh, I don't know,' she said, gazing off at

some horses in a far-off field. 'People misunderstand each other, they imagine all kinds of things about what the other person wants, and then pretty soon they're strangers.' She paused a moment, took a drag. 'What surprised me was that you never put up a fight for him. It was as if you expected him to leave you.'

For some reason this brought tears to my eyes. 'But Doris, it just happened. He stopped caring for me. It wasn't my fault.'

'I know,' she said, without conviction.

I was frantic. 'Why would I want him to leave me? How can you say that?'

'Look, I'm sorry. Forget it.'

But she had already planted the idea in my head. 'No, Doris, tell me what I did wrong.'

'It doesn't matter, does it? It all happened a long time ago.'

For a moment, I wanted to argue with her. But I understood, as I might not have been able to in our old lives, that she was only trying to help. Perhaps I *had* driven him away—or circumstances had.

'What should I do now? Write a letter?' I asked, with something tender in my voice.

'Yes, but you also need to do some research,' she took her last swig of beer. 'I mean, does he really feel this way, or does he feel this way because his marriage is falling apart and you've come to symbolize something for him?'

'That's the million-dollar question, isn't it?'

'What is it you really want, Frannie? Would marry him in a minute?'

'I have no idea,' I said. I didn't want to let on how much, at this moment, I believed that

85

letter. Little scenes from an imaginary future kept appearing to me. *I'm standing at the stove and Peter holds me from behind, resting his chin on my shoulder; we're sitting on the rocks over the river; it's night, and he's unpinning my bun and combing his fingers through the twists of my hair.*

'Well,' Doris said, taking a drag and squinting one eye against the smoke, 'let's say his intentions are honorable, just for the sake of argument. Would you marry him, Frannie?' Her voice was flat, too flat, and I wondered whether she was afraid of being left alone.

'I really don't know. I'm not even sure when I'll feel like writing to him. I don't want to yet. Right now, I just want to enjoy our trip. Don't worry, Doris, I won't up and leave you.'

'Look, you do whatever you want,' she snapped. 'Have I ever held you back?'

'No,' I said. 'I'm sorry. I just thought, well, if you were the one who'd gotten this letter, I'd probably feel awfully jealous. I'd be so afraid of losing you.'

'I appreciate your concern.' Doris stood up, slapping at her skirt to smooth it out, 'but for one thing, I'm certain I'll never lose you—you're too tenacious for that, Frannie, even married. I really think it'd be wonderful if it worked out. Now, do you want another beer?'

'No thanks.' I watched her as she disappeared through the glass door into the house. It was one of those rare moments when I had absolutely no idea what she was thinking.

*

ANNIE'S HUSBAND WAS late, and we held up dinner for him. As she pinched some tinfoil over the top of the serving dish and put it back in the oven she said, 'Poor Chuck. They never let him out on time.'

After an hour or so, the door banged open, and a tall man—still handsome despite his paunch and thinning hair—strode into the living room. I was sitting on the couch, a book on my lap, and he stared at me as if I'd snuck into the house. 'Who are you?'

I started to explain, but he interrupted. 'That's right—she told me.' Then he barked in the direction of the kitchen: 'I've had a hell of a day. Annie? Are you there?' He stood where he was, his arms crossed, waiting.

Annie rushed into the room and handed him a drink. 'Now, come on,' she said. 'We've held dinner long enough.'

We sat down to eat at a mahogany table with magnificent, ornate silverware. The effect was ruined, however, by an old saddle thrown over the chair in the corner and the yellow shag rug, which was covered with dog hair.

Chuck leaned toward Doris and asked, 'What do you think of Memphis?'

'It's a beautiful city. But I'm sorry to say it does have a bad reputation up North. All we've heard lately is about the riot where the police shot the negroes.'

Chuck had drunk two quick whiskeys by now. 'Oh, you have no idea what we've had to put up with down here.' He said this last word as if it had two syllables: *he-ah*. 'I don't know why I bother to pay my taxes. All those trashmen think they're too good for decent work.'

The daughter, Peg—a rangy girl with reddish brown hair—narrowed her eyes at him. 'Don't you even care what those poor people have been going through?'

'Oh *shush*, Peg,' Annie said. 'Your father's sloshed. Don't pay him any mind.'

'Peggy,' he said, in a quiet voice that I hadn't heard before, 'you just don't understand. It's easy to say I should be throwing all my money at them, but you try working as hard as I do and see how it feels.'

'*You, you, you*—that's all you know about.' Peg was pushing her chair away from the table, ready to storm out.

Annie put her hand on Peg's arm. 'Honey, instead of sinking to your father's level, why don't you just humor him? Now,' she said, looking around the table, 'who would like some of the delicious jello salad Frannie made?' Annie was raised in Texas, and she used her charm like a blunt object.

After dinner, she insisted on doing the dishes. Doris and I sat out on the porch to enjoy the cooler air. We'd only been out there a few minutes when the glass door slid open and closed again, and Peg came out. She leaned against the railing beside us.

'Can I bum a cigarette?' she said to Doris. 'I'm dying.'

Doris passed her the pack.

'Doris!' I hissed, but she ignored me.

Peg lit up and took a drag, and then let her

head loll backward as she blew out the smoke. 'I hate him,' she said.

'Well,' Doris said, 'your father's not the most tactful man, but he must love you very much. And your mother's a wonderful person.'

'My mom's OK,' she said, 'but she never stands up to him. It makes me sick.' She took another drag and then flicked her ashes like a practiced smoker. 'I'm going to go live in New York, and I'm never coming back. Randy, my boyfriend, he's going to go to Columbia. Dad hates him.'

I felt awkward, hearing all these things I shouldn't, but Doris didn't seem to mind. She said, 'You're going to be a senior in high school this fall?'

'Yeah,' Peg said. She was sitting up on the railing, her freckled legs dangling.

'Well, then,' Doris said. 'You only have a year. It's not so bad.'

'Yeah, right,' Peg said. 'A year of torture.'

'You're lucky, really. You're going to go to college, aren't you?'

'I guess,' Peg said.

'Well, Frannie and I never went. We stayed home and helped our father with his business, and then we took care of him when he got sick. Now how would you like that?'

'Doris, don't make it sound so awful.' My voice was thin, whiny, in the dark. 'Dad always said that if one of us wanted to go to college, he'd find a way. We chose our lives.'

'We didn't exactly *choose* what happened,' she said. 'We just sort of hung around waiting to get married. I don't think either of us expected it to take

89

so long. But you know, girls were encouraged to be very passive back then. See how lucky you are, Peg?'

Peg swung her legs as she considered this. 'Yeah,' she said. 'But I still have to wait a year.'

Doris leaned against the railing, putting her arm around Peg. 'In a year, you can go have the most marvelous adventures. Think about that,' she said.

They both fell quiet, then, blowing out smoke and gazing up at the stars. The bugs—creaking and chirping and buzzing—swelled to fill our silence. I remembered how, as a child, Doris told me the high-pitched click of the crickets came from the stars, and how I believed her like I always believed everything she told me.

'But what'll I do when Randy leaves?' Peg said in a small voice.

'Well, you'll write to him.' Doris tightened her arm around Peg. 'And, quite possibly, you'll find some other boy who you like even better.'

It was unlike Doris to be so familiar with someone she barely knew—even with a younger cousin. I wondered if she did it to make me jealous, to shut me out. I leaned against the cool of the glass door and watched them together, wishing she had been like that for me. As Doris lit another cigarette for Peg—their faces almost identical in the sudden flare—I understood how it would be from now on.

PERHAPS BECAUSE I was sleeping on the lumpy fold-out sofa in the living room—or maybe it was drinking the beer—that night I had a strange dream. It started off as any spinster's dream would, with worries about change lost and trains missed. But suddenly it shifted: I was underwater, arms and legs and torsos and heads floating all around me. The limbs trailed beads of blood. They brushed against me as cold and intent as fish. They caressed one another, severed hand sliding longingly over a leg.

I woke in a sweat and had to turn on the light, but even then I couldn't dispel my dread. I took out Peter's letter again and read it through, and in my state it seemed to whisper of perverse desires.

I longed for my father then, to show him the letter. Oh dear, uncritical Dad—he would have looked at it and said, 'Why this is wonderful, absolutely wonderful.'

I gathered my legs up in my arms, put my chin on my knees, and tried to picture him on a good day from last year. He'd be sitting in the chair by his window with a book or a newspaper, his shirt starched crisp and his legs crossed at the ankle. I'd bring him a glass of juice with some medicine. He'd make a joke. 'Ah the pills. Now where shall I hide them today after you leave?'

I held onto this image, trying to bring his face, his hands, into focus, trying to feel again the mood of humorous good will he exuded. But memory doesn't work that way. Instead, another scene came back to me vividly: Doris and I walking across the thick, hushed carpets of the funeral home, a man in his Sunday suit ushering us among the caskets. We feigned interest in the mahogany and brass, the satin and silverplate. But when we looked at those yawning caskets, we could only think about how soon they'd shut the lid on him.

One of us had to identify the body. Doris

91

volunteered, but I said no, I'd do it. I didn't want it to be like when Mom died—all so unreal. She was fretting over a lost earring one afternoon, as alive as anyone, and then several days later we were marching past her casket in church. She had been Methodist, and so the lid on the casket stayed down. I had stared at that white, shiny box all through the service, but I couldn't convince myself she was inside. I think that made my grief harder in the end.

So now I wanted to see Dad. Doris stayed in the showroom and I followed the plump, somber man through a dark door. He stopped about halfway across the room from my father, and I stood beside him. They'd laid Dad out in a pine box and put a sheet over everything but his face. I noticed his skin had turned gray and his cheeks had sunk in.

'Do you identify this man as your father? If so, could you print his name here?' the man said.

'Yes.' I took the clipboard and filled it in. Afterward, I wanted to cross the room and hover over the box to scrutinize the body, touch its skin—so I could understand exactly what death took away and what it left behind.

But the plump man was already leaving. 'This way, please,' he said, and I followed dutifully.

It was propriety that made me walk away from death. And for months after, it was propriety that kept me from really examining his death in my imagination. I could picture my father's body as it had looked that day, of course—but when I tried to get any closer to the truth of it, to think about what his death meant, something, some mental equivalent of that plump undertaker maybe, pushed me away.

Now, though, I was beginning to understand my father's death—I mean, my feelings about it. Of course, I had been devastated. Of course I missed him terribly. But something else, too. When I'd come home after the funeral, exhausted from mourning, I'd stepped into the house and thought, *Mine*. Even when I'd been cleaning out his drawers (wanting to cry because of the familiar smell), I'd thought *Mine*—and also when I touched his tin box, *Mine*, when I dusted the picture of my mother, *Mine* when I turned on the lamp near the sofa . . . I hate to think how these niggardly hallelujahs rang in my head.

Of course, what I really meant was not *mine*, and *mine* and *mine*—for I didn't care about owning these knickknacks, not really. But when I could hold his tin box in my fist, when could I open it and see what he'd hidden inside (shirt stays, a safety clip, two pink pills), that was the moment when I realized how free I was. I was no longer a daughter; I was something else entirely.

PETER'S LETTER—IT burned like a hot little fire of possibility in my purse. It made me do crazy things. The next day, I'd gone into town to pick up some groceries for Annie, but as I walked out of the Piggly Wiggly, I caught sight of a beauty parlor as pink as a birthday cake. I crossed the street to look at its window display, which couldn't have changed in many years: the pictures of women with bouffants and bubble cuts had faded, and the displays of brushes and shampoos were covered in dust. Something about its air of neglect appealed to me; without thinking, I walked in.

The place was empty, but smelled reassuringly of chemicals, which I remembered from girlhood trips to the beauty parlor with my mother. An older woman, scrawny, wearing polyester pants, appeared out of a back room. 'Well, hello,' she said, wiping her hands. '*My*, aren't you a pretty thing! Sit down.'

'Oh, I'm not sure I want anything done,' I said, shifting the groceries to my other arm.

'Of course you do,' she said. She closed her eyes, as if consulting some inner vision. 'I see it,' she said, eyes still closed. 'Just a little longer than your shoulders, very straight, and brightened up. Yes— we'd have to brighten it.'

'Well, that's not exactly what I had in mind . . .' my voice trailed off. Now I didn't know why I'd walked in. I felt bad about wasting her time.

'Just sit down and let me see what kind of hair you have.' And, under her spell, I did.

Hovering behind me, she removed all the pins and stays, so my hair fell down my back. 'Look at this! You should be showing it off,' she scolded. Though she kept her own hair in tight and unflattering curls, I trusted her. 'It's just a shade away from being red, you know,' she added.

'It is?' I leaned forward and squinted at myself in the mirror, but my hair, still showing folds where it had been pinned up so long, was only as it had always been, the brownish color of spinster's speckles, as I've heard age spots called.

'First we'll wash it, and bring out some of that color—then we'll go to work,' she said.

'I washed it this morning,' I began to protest, but she already had the plastic bib around me and was leading me over to the chairs that leaned into sinks.

She sat me down and began working. I liked the feel of the water brushing my hair back, but when I smelled the peroxide in the steam, I jerked my head up. 'What are you doing?'

'Just putting in a little color,' she said and pushed me back down into the water.

'No, don't—please!'

'Too late, Honey,' she said with a satisfied air.

When it came to cutting, she was just as impossible. I said that I wanted something I could still put up in a bun, if need be, but she persevered: 'Hair like that, so straight, you want to show it off. Other women are ironing theirs these days just to get what you have naturally. I'm going to cut it here,' she scissored my wet hair with her fingers. 'It'll be *very* French.'

When she had cut and clipped and dried my hair, it fell just past my jaw, straight and thick and shining like copper.

'Oh no,' I said. 'This won't do. I can't go outside with my hair this color. You have to dye it brown again, right away.'

'But that would damage it, hon. Look, gals are often a little shocked at first. But then they *all* come back and tell me how much they love it. So give it a week—if you don't like it, I'll dye it back for free.'

'I doubt I'll be here in a week.'

'Now, don't get angry on me. I really thought you'd be tickled. It seems to me you're awfully pretty like that, but if you're upset, why, it's on the house.'

I paid anyway and walked out feeling bad for the way I'd raised my voice at her. At the same time, I was terribly angry, especially when I stopped before a mirror in the window of a drug store. In the sun, my hair was the color of a hussy's lips, a hickey, a new scar. When I leaned forward, it fell in hooks around my face, so that I had to swipe it back. There was no putting it up, out of my face, anymore. I got into the car and jammed the key into the ignition, but then slumped over the steering wheel and cried. Suddenly, I was horribly tired of this new life. I just wanted to look like myself. I wanted my old clothes back, but Doris had convinced me to give them to the Goodwill in Nashville. I wanted to be sitting on my bed in our house listening to the rattle of the train far away, measuring the afternoon by the slow travel of sun across the floor. And for the first time, I realized that the old Frannie in her room with the clove balls hanging in the closets and the loud tick of the wind-up clock, that Frannie was gone forever. Now I was a woman with red hair.

Chapter Seven

DORIS LOVED IT, of course. She and Annie gushed about how the cut flattered my face, how I had the natural coloring to carry it off.

'There *is* red in the family—Doris and Peggy both,' Annie said.

'Well, it's driving me half crazy, the way it's always swinging in my face,' I said. I was holding a hand mirror and bobby-pinning the thick red ropes of hair onto the top of my head, a simulation of a bun.

'Oh, don't listen to her,' Doris said to Annie. 'She just wants to complain, but she'll come around.' Annie, sitting next to me on the couch, placed a warm, damp hand on my arm. 'I know how you feel. I've had haircuts that just about did me in.'

'It's really kind of amazing,' Doris said, 'I mean, you look like an entirely different person.'

'Stop it. I want to look like me.'

'Well, let's just forget it,' Annie said. 'I'm

going to make more coffee.' With a huff of effort, she got up.

When she'd gone, Doris leaned forward and said in a near whisper, 'Don't you think it's getting time to leave? Don't you want to go somewhere?' She was curled up in a formal living room chair, the wooden Chinese screen behind her making her face look white and severe.

'Yes,' I said, 'home.' I'd been peevish all day, because of the haircut.

She laughed. 'You can't go *home*. Peter will hear you're back and want to see you. Unless I'm mistaken, you're not ready for that yet.'

I sucked in my breath. 'That's right. Peter. We can't go back there, Doris, can we? What are we going to do?'

'Listen, I have an idea.' She compulsively reached in her purse for her cigarettes and then remembered she couldn't smoke inside. She had that look on her face like she needed a cigarette badly. 'Let's go see old Uncle Jack down in Texas. We're almost there already.'

'All right,' I said. To me, Uncle Jack's farm was a forbidden paradise—the place Doris went that one summer while I had to stay in New Hampshire. How I remembered those letters she'd sent back that smelled sweetly of grass and outdoors. She wore her cousin's cowboy hat and rode a pony with a white star on his face; she went to church with them and made eyes at the boy who always sat across the aisle. Doris came back from that summer a different girl, tan and tall.

'Uncle Jack was so sweet to me,' she said.

'I've always wanted to see him again . . . We could take Peggy, too. She'd like to visit her grandpa, don't you think?'

'Peggy? No, we can't do that.' Something about Doris's enthusiasm put me on guard.

'Of course we can. She's been begging me to come with us.'

'She has?'

'You missed the whole scene this morning. I told Annie I'd been wanting to see Uncle Jack, and once Peggy got wind that we might leave, all hell broke lose. She managed to pick a fight with Annie, even though Annie didn't seem to care if she went with us. In fact, I think Annie would *love* it if we took Peg off her hands.'

'Oh dear,' I said. 'How would we ever keep her under control?'

'She'll be fine.' Doris waved her hand in front of her as if brushing away my objections. Somehow, that gesture settled it between us.

WE LEFT THE next morning. Doris and I had the car packed by eight, and then found out that Peg hadn't even gotten up. As we waited for her, Doris said, 'We're traveling with a teenager now. We're going to have to make some adjustments.' Finally, Peg ran out of the house wearing flip-flops and cutoff jeans, her hair up in a messy ponytail.

'Don't you need more than that?' I asked, when I saw that all she had with her was a knapsack.

'Oh, this is plenty,' she said as she climbed into the back seat.

We all waved good-bye to Annie, who was

standing in the yard in slippers and a nightgown. As soon we were out of sight, Peg draped herself over the back of our seat so that her head and arms hung between Doris and me.

'I'm dying for a cigarette, Aunt Doris. Please, pretty please.'

'In my purse,' said Doris, who was driving. 'And don't call me *aunt*, remember?'

'Doris, we're going to have to lay down some rules,' I said. I didn't like sounding cross, but I felt we owed that to Annie—not letting Peg smoke.

She lit the cigarette, her head still hanging over the back of our seat. 'Take a left at the next light,' she said.

'Frannie, we're not her parents,' Doris said. 'It's simply up to us to make sure she has a good time and doesn't get hurt. Her moral character is her own business.'

'Keep going straight,' Peg said.

'Well, at least blow that smoke out the window, not in my face,' I said. I knew I should make more of a fuss, for Annie's sake, but an odd calm was settling over me. I found myself justifying our laxness: Would forbidding her to smoke really work anyway? Hadn't she started long before she met us?

Suddenly Peg yelled, 'Stop, stop! Doris, stop!' Doris slammed on the brakes.

'It's right here. I'll just be a minute.' She climbed out of the car and ran up to one of the houses along the street.

'Please don't be angry, Fran,' Doris said, undoing her seatbelt and turning toward me. 'Peg's going to bring a friend.'

The way she said it, my stomach hurt.
'What friend?'

'Her boyfriend.'

'Have you gone crazy?'

'Look, Frannie, calm down—it's only for a day. He just wants to come with us today, and then wherever we end up tonight, he'll take the bus back from there.'

'Annie doesn't know about this, does she?'

'What's to know?'

I was about to answer when Peg's boyfriend climbed into the car.

'Doris, Aunt Fran,' Peg said, 'this is Randy.'

'We still haven't discussed this,' I said. 'Nobody told me he was coming.'

Randy looked at me sheepishly. He had hair past his ears, wore wire-frame glasses and a string of beads around his neck, and he smelled of . . . well, perhaps that was my imagination. 'I don't mean to cause any trouble,' he said in a soft voice.

Peg threw her arms around him. 'He's *got* to come with us! He's going away to college in less than a month, and I'm never going to see him.'

'Peg, for heaven's sake,' I said. 'Please calm down and let me think.' But I couldn't. Or rather, I knew I should have made a scene—the old Frannie would have—but I couldn't work up the moral indignation required. When it came down to it, I really didn't care what happened, as long as I didn't get in trouble with Annie later. 'The fact of the matter is,' I said to Doris, 'we'd be lying to Annie. So we could solve this right now by telling her that Randy's going to come along for the day.'

I turned to look at them in the back seat. Peg had her hand clamped around Randy's tan arm. He gazed at me solemnly. His unlined face still had about it the tender seriousness of adolescence.

'Aunt Frannie,' Peg said. 'There's no way Mom's going to say yes, because she's afraid of what Dad would say, and Dad would never say yes because he's such a jerk.'

Doris shook her head wearily. 'Frannie, it's just for the day. Stop making a scene.'

'Oh, all right,' I sighed. 'I guess it can't do any harm. But no funny business, because if Chuck ever finds out about this, there'll be hell to pay.'

'Thanks, Aunt Fran.' Peg grabbed me from behind, her arms clasped a minute around my neck, her cheek brushing against mine.

I held the map on my knee and directed Doris to Route 40. When I saw we were heading for the bridge over the Mississippi, I got strangely nervous, and my stomach tightened again. The river lay low in its banks, glittering dangerously, the halfway mark of our nation. As Doris sped onto the bridge and the sound of the tires changed, I thought the river under us looked like a line someone had dared us to cross.

Chapter Eight

AT SOME POINT Doris suggested we stop for food; Randy cleared his throat and shyly said, 'I packed lunch, if you all want it. Nothing special—Cokes and sandwiches. But I thought I'd bring something, you know, as a way of thanking you.'

'See,' Peg said. 'See how nice he is?'

We decided on a picnic, and spread out a blanket on the grass near a rest stop in Arkansas. The land stretched so flat you could just make out the horizon, where the farmhouses became as tiny as Monopoly pieces. We ate without saying much—instead, we gazed off at the miniature lives spread all around us, the silos and cornfields and barns. After lunch, we played Concentration with the old deck of cards Doris and I kept in the glove compartment. It was the scenic-waterfall deck, missing the three of spades. I remembered banishing it to the car years ago.

After the game, as Doris packed our things back into the car, I went into the bathroom to wash up. Peg followed me through the door and grabbed my arm. 'Isn't he great, Aunt Frannie?'

'He seems very nice . . . very quiet.'

Peg stood before the mirror, fixing her ponytail. 'Yeah, sometimes I wonder what he's thinking.'

'Why don't you ask him?' I said. We walked outside.

'I do, but he doesn't tell me. Look at him.' Randy was leaning against the car, leafing through a newspaper. 'Always reading.' She bounded over to him and put her arm around his shoulder, nearly knocking him off balance. 'What's up?'

'The Republican convention,' he said.

She laughed. 'I didn't mean that. I meant, are you and Doris ready to leave?'

'Yeah, sure.' He smiled at her, though I thought he seemed a little annoyed.

Really, I didn't mind Randy. But his presence made Peg intolerable. She became loud, almost hysterical, whenever he stopped paying attention to her. But at least things would be better once Randy went home. Toward evening, we began seeing signs for Texas. 'Well, I believe the best place to stay tonight would be somewhere near the border, maybe Texarcana,' I said in a cheerful voice, turning to look in the back seat. 'Randy could get the bus there.'

Peg gazed at me, silent.

After a minute Doris said, 'I made that up, Fran. We never planned to have him take the bus. He's coming with us, all the way.'

'What do you mean you made that up?' I

asked icily. She drove without looking over at me, steering with one hand.

'I knew you needed some time to get used to the idea, so, I don't know, I said that. It just came out.'

'You've never done that to me before—tricked me.'

I sounded so hurt that she had to glance over at me. 'All right. I'm sorry. I shouldn't have lied to you. Do you want Randy to go home on the bus? Shush, Peg, I'll handle this. Do you? We can just drop him right off if you say the word.'

'Why are you making me the villain? *I* wasn't the one who promised he could come along.'

Peg touched me on the shoulder, and I turned to look at her. 'I'm really sorry, Aunt Fran,' she said. Unlike Doris, she seemed to mean it. 'I begged Aunt Doris to do this. I don't want you two to fight about it. It's my fault.'

105

Randy said, 'I'll go home. I don't mind catching the bus,' his eyes on the floor. I thought he wanted to cry.

'Look,' I said, 'you seem like a very nice young man. I have no objection to you personally. I just think it's wrong to lie to Annie. Now, if someone promises to call her and explain, things will be fine.'

'All right,' Doris said, tossing her cigarette out the window, 'as soon as we get to the motel I'll call her myself. No big deal.'

'Good,' I said.

A half hour or so later, she pulled off the highway. The motel lot was empty, save for one or two cars, and she drove over to the edge and parked next to a long field. We all sat for a moment staring out at the tickling of the scrub grass in the wind, and beyond, the bright blue roof of a Howard Johnson's. I listened to the ticks of the cooling engine. After the movement of the highway, it was stillness that seemed a miracle, each stone and stalk of grass as mysteriously inert as a monument. It gave me a chill down my back to think of all the objects in this world like bent hairpins and lost buttons that stayed put—in the bottoms of drawers or the corners of rooms—all the things I'd shed without remembering them. I'd always thought of myself as somehow belonging with those objects that sat and gathered dust. But now I'd become another kind of thing entirely; I'd gotten used to the highway.

Doris slapped the steering wheel. 'OK, I'll go into the office, call Annie, and get the room keys.'

'Wonderful,' I said—feeling guilty now that I'd made such a fuss—and got out of the car to stretch.

Doris came back after fifteen minutes or so. 'Well,' she said, 'I explained that we had a stowaway, and I offered to send him home, but she said, no, it would be all right as long as Chuck never finds out. Oh, yes, and we're supposed to act as chaperones for the kids, keep them apart.' She laughed. 'But what she doesn't know won't hurt her.' All the while, she had been jiggling her hand, making the room keys jangle together.

'All right,' I said. 'Then let's give Randy his own room and the three of us can share.'

'No.' She pitched one of the keys to Peg. 'This is for the kids.'

'*Cool!*' Peg said, and she and Randy grabbed their knapsacks and disappeared around the side of the motel.

'Oh, Lord.' I was leaning against the car and I put my hands over my face.

'Calm down, Fran,' Doris said.

'Don't patronize me. You promised Annie we'd keep them apart, and now you want me to help you deceive her?'

'Oh, for God's sake,' Doris said. 'What else do you want me to do? They'd just sneak out and meet each other if I hadn't. This way they'll stay put.'

'Well, Doris, that's a fine way of making them stay put.'

She sighed. 'I had a talk with Peg. It's not anything they haven't done before.'

I suppose I turned a little pale.

'Fran,' she said, 'it's different these days. I'm sorry if you don't like that, but the world has just gone and changed on us.'

'I know why you're doing this—you're mad at me because I got that letter from Peter.' My voice was cold, quiet. 'You're trying to punish me. That's it, isn't it?'

'Oh, come on, Frannie.' She put her hands on her hips, making our key jingle. 'It has nothing to do with you.'

'Then I don't understand. Because you barely know Peg, and here you are bending to her every whim.'

She turned from me and hefted her suitcase out of the trunk. It was still light out, the reddish light of the evening, and birds swooped overhead.

Doris sat down on her suitcase, as if she were too tired to move, and gave the motel balcony where the kids had gone a glance. Then she said, 'Why do you think? I want her to have everything I missed, all the freedom I never had.'

'Do you really think you're helping her? What if she gets pregnant?'

'Don't worry. That's taken care of.'

'Oh Lord, Doris. I don't know what to say to you. This whole thing's so crazy. Do you want to make her like you, running around with men? Is that what you want?'

'You just don't get it, do you?' Doris jumped off her suitcase and took a few steps toward me, squinting in her fury. 'We can't all turn ourselves off like you do, Frannie, while we wait for marriage. Maybe you aren't even waiting for marriage anymore—maybe you don't want men in your life at all. But *I* sure as hell do. Look,' she continued, calming down a little. 'I don't see what possible harm this can do to Peg. You want her to run off and get married like her mother did? I think it's better this way.'

'All right, fine. But that's not the point. Whatever you want for Peg, well, I'll try to understand. But I don't want you lying to me. You know you've been treating me like dirt.'

'I'm sorry you think that.' I could see by the set of her jaw that she wasn't sorry at all. 'But what else could I do, Frannie? Everything becomes such an issue with you. I know you're going to get mad at me for saying this, but I'm tired of your prudishness.'

I shook my head, wanting to cry. 'Maybe

I'm not as much of a prude as you think, Doris. Maybe I'm changing. You could at least treat me decently. And sometimes what you call prudishness is just common sense.'

'All right, I'm sorry,' she said angrily, picking up her suitcase. 'I'm going up to the room.'

LATER THAT EVENING, I stole one of Doris's cigarettes out of the car and went up to stand on the balcony. We weren't speaking and I wanted to wait until she fell asleep before I came back to the room.

Earlier, I'd forced myself to knock on the kids' door and see if they wanted anymore to eat or perhaps the bar of soap we kept tied up in a plastic bag. After some time, the door had opened a crack and a flushed Peg had said, 'No thanks, Aunt Fran. We're just fine.'

'All right, then,' I'd said, my own face burning. I thought about that as I leaned against the railing over on the other side of the motel. That girl was half my age. I had always been proud of my virginity, especially as compared to Doris, who to be fair, hadn't given in until her late twenties, I guess.

I knew when it happened, because she had called and told me, with no embarrassment at all, that she wouldn't be home that night. 'I didn't want you to wait up for me,' she'd said. She didn't say anything about Dad, but I knew I'd have to lie to him. I came up with something about Doris staying with friends in the country, a drive that was better made in the morning. Dad nodded and went back to his paper,

109

not realizing that this night meant a subtle shift, forever, in our lives.

This happened during the first blush of my love for Peter. That particular night, he came over, and we took a long walk. While we strolled beside the moonlit road—which still smelled of the day, of tar and burnt oil—I had imagined Doris with her beau, whichever one it was then. I pictured her calmly lifting a glass to her mouth and saying, 'I suppose I will stay over.' She wouldn't have decided in the midst of passion, but long before. And she wouldn't be nervous—not Doris. She would look him straight in the eye and say, 'It's time I tried it.'

I pictured all this as I walked beside Peter, we didn't dare to do much more than hold hands. Back then, I'd been smug, thinking I would soon marry this man—and after we'd chosen the pattern for our silverware and plates, and after we'd wed in a Quaker ceremony and written every last thank you note to every relative and our new house was spotless with each piece of china in the cabinet—only then would I be ready to give myself to Peter. But never, I imagined, would I do it in the desperate way that Doris chose.

I LIT THE cigarette as I'd seen people in movies do, cupping my hand around it, so that the match illuminated my palm like a whole little world. I sucked on the filter, and the flame lept to the tip of the cigarette. Then I let the match fall to the concrete walk a story below where I was standing on the motel balcony. Out beyond the parking lot, cars passed with swishes along the highway. Once in a while, there was a long, low groan, and then a rumble, and an eighteen-wheeler would roll solemnly past, a string of lights along its side. The cigarette smoked silently in my hand without my having to do anything but hold it.

I was still proud of my virginity, my absolute and unsullied spinsterhood. But truth be told, I was also weary of it, especially with the warm breeze of that night on my bare arms and two teenagers a few hundred feet away doing things I was trying not to imagine. My eyes fastened then on the phone booth to one side of the parking lot, beside some dark gas pumps. It alone was lit up—over its door was an unearthly white sign with a blue phone receiver on it.

Without really thinking, I walked down the stairs and across the parking lot, and I found myself inside the booth. I closed the door and a fan came on. I still remembered the number—I've always had a head for numbers. I fed the phone with change that I'd collected in my purse for tolls. If Eva answered, I figured, I could always hang up.

But Peter answered. 'Hello?' he said with a dead sound to his voice, or so I imagined.

'Peter, it's me, Frannie.'

'Frannie,' his voice changed, became urgent. 'Did you get my letter?'

'Yes, I got it. I liked it very much.'

'Where are you?' He sounded frightened.

'In Arkansas. I'm at a phone booth in the middle of nowhere. It's a little eerie.' I didn't feel nervous talking to him, not exactly. But his voice gave me that old jolt I remembered, the queasy stomach.

111

'Are you all right?' he said.

'Yes, of course. I just thought I'd call. Can you talk? Is she there?'

'She's out. She's always out. You have no idea, Frannie . . .'

'No, I guess I don't.' I noticed that my cigarette had gone out. I dropped it on the floor of the phone booth.

'I'm sorry,' he said.

'Don't be sorry. It's just that I can't get a fix on you. What does your house look like now? What are you wearing?'

'The place is a mess and I'm a mess. I've started drinking. I drink a few bourbons and I read Flaubert and feel sorry for myself.'

'Don't you have any friends who can help you?'

'No,' he said, his voice wavering. 'They're all her friends, Fran. She's filing for divorce.'

'I thought you wanted the divorce.' Normally, I wouldn't have pried, but he sounded too lost to care.

'We both wanted a divorce.' I heard the ice clink in his glass as he took a sip. 'I just couldn't bear to do it. She's looking for a place now.'

'Oh, dear,' I said. 'You have to take care of yourself.'

'Please come home, Frannie.' He was on the verge of tears now.

'Look, I care about you very much, but I'm not going to pick up the pieces. I have more sense than that.'

A recorded voice came on, saying I had to

deposit more money. 'I have to go, Peter. I'll call you again soon.'

'No—wait.'

'What?'

'Please, don't hang up.'

'I have to hang up sometime,' I said, exasperated but also flattered.

'I've ruined my chances with you, haven't I?'

'No. It's just that I have to go. I'll call you later.' The phone clicked and went dead and I didn't know whether he had heard me.

I TURNED THE key in the latch as quietly as possible. It was dark in the room, but when I closed the door behind me, I heard the shift of sheets as Doris sat up in bed.

113

'I'm sorry, Frannie,' she said. 'I didn't mean to get so upset with you before. You're right—I shouldn't have lied to you.'

'Forget about it,' I said, unzipping my dress.

'It's just that with Peggy I have a soft spot, you know?' I heard her voice catch. 'I want to make it easier for her than it was for me.'

I pulled my nightgown over my head and tucked some wayward hair behind my ears. 'Do you really think you're making it easier?' I said. 'I guess we'll never agree about that.'

'No, I guess we won't. But maybe that's OK.' I heard her fumbling for something on the nightstand. A match flared, and for a minute I saw her face in the orange glow. She was looking down at the cigarette, sucking in with a tremendous contentment. The match went out, and Doris became a dot of light on the other side of the room. 'You know,' she said, exhaling, 'sometimes I think you get upset about things—like Peggy being with Randy—just because you feel like you're obliged to, for propriety's sake. Deep down, though, I think you don't give a damn.'

I sat down on my bed, Indian style. 'Yes,' I said, 'maybe you're right. It's all become much too tiring. Better not to think about it.'

Doris smoked silently for a minute. 'Frannie,' she said finally, 'you must have strong . . . desires sometimes. We've never talked about it—isn't that strange? I want to know how you stand it, having desire and no man.' I heard her settle further over toward her corner, because she felt awkward about asking such a question.

114

I was blushing in the dark, thinking maybe she could tell I'd just called Peter, that perhaps something in my voice or manner betrayed it. But that was impossible.

'Desire?' I said, as if I didn't understand. Our lives back in New Hampshire, the narrow hallways of our house, the air crisp as a cold apple, the long evenings of backgammon—all of this had made it impossible to speak about things like desire, as if there were no room for it in the house, or perhaps no time. But here we were, all the time in the world, all the space of an anonymous motel room.

'Yes. Desire,' she said, caressing the word with her voice. 'For instance, when you were with Peter, didn't you get carried away sometimes? Or want to get carried away?'

I breathed out a long, resigned sigh. 'Peter and I were waiting until we got married. We never exactly talked about it, but he was careful not to push me into anything I wasn't comfortable with. That was a relief.'

'But sometimes you wanted to just let loose, didn't you?' she asked, determined.

'I'm not like you. I was happy to wait. I loved having him kiss me, but that was all I wanted right then.'

'I can't just kiss a man and be done. I don't think it's even the sex. I just want something exciting to happen . . . Oh, Frannie, is that so bad?'

'It gets you into trouble.'

'Yes,' she said, 'that it does.' She fell silent; eventually I heard her lie down. 'Well, I can't figure it out now,' she said. 'Goodnight.'

I said goodnight but lay awake, a bundle of nerves. I had been terribly on edge as we talked—so afraid she'd see through me. I did have urges, though I had never admitted them to anyone, not even Doris. My urges, nursed in secret, had taken root in some hidden part of my heart, like the stunted things that grow under a layer of leaves in the forest.

When did it start? It started with the red Mutascope. This ancient machine—there probably aren't any left anymore—looked like a Victorian post-box, all covered with metal scrollwork. You stood on a little stool, dropped a penny in the slot and put your eyes up to a visor. Inside, you saw a short cartoon, usually something brief and whimsical—a dog chasing a cat, a monkey doing tricks.

I'm not explaining it right. The cartoons weren't like the ones you'd see before a feature movie. Really, the machine was just a glorified flipbook. It had a metal arm that shuffled a stack of pictures so quickly that they seemed to form one picture, a simple drawing that moved in the jerky way of a silent film.

As a girl, I loved those machines. My mother had explained that before motion pictures the Mutascopes were everywhere—in drugstores next to the weight-and-fate machines or out in front of soda fountains. When I was a girl, though, the only ones left were in the most broken-down arcades at the boardwalk.

My passion for the Mutascope was so great that one time I even ran away from my parents at the beach and went traipsing along the boardwalk. Finally, in a dark building where men stood serious before the pinging and clatter of the pinball machines, I found one, red as a fire hydrant, except for the dirt and grit clogging its filigreed iron. It had no stool, so I had to stand on my tiptoes and stretch my arm high to drop in the penny.

I had been expecting a cartoon, of course. But instead of drawings, this machine had photographs—real people, a man and a woman. In the panic of flipping pictures, they lost their clothes and fell to the floor together. What shocked me was not so much their violent mashing but the strangeness of their adult bodies: the sag of their flesh and the patches of hair on them.

The machine groaned and turned dark. I glanced around guiltily, knowing I'd seen something I shouldn't have. None of the men had noticed me, though—so I put another penny in, and another, and another. It wasn't prurience, but a fascination at the topsy-turvy world inside the Mutascope. I was eight.

The year I turned thirteen, I shot up several inches all at once. During that time, I lived in my body as I never had before—examining the hairs that sprouted under my arms, staring at my own eyes in the mirror, touching the new dollops of fat on my chest. I watched other peoples' bodies, too: the damp spot on my mother's dress after she washed the dishes and the way the fabric clung to the small pillow of her stomach; my father's ankles, so smooth that I wondered if his socks had worn all the hair away.

A boy in my class had ears that stuck out. They glowed pink when he stood in front of the window. He was a boastful, stupid boy, but I fell in love with his ears and I imagined kissing them, running my finger over the soft ridges of his lobes. I must have sat for a whole hour once just fondling those ears in my imagination. Soon I craved more, but I knew so little about what went on between men and women that it was impossible to titillate myself. That's when I remembered the Mutascope.

117

I had a whole dirty movie stored in my mind, and I'd never used it! That very afternoon, I ran up to the attic, crammed myself into the farthest corner, closed my eyes, and waited for the movie to play in my mind. But it didn't work like that, of course—I could only recall the barest fragments, the dimmest bits of what I'd seen years ago. So I had to reconstruct the pornographic movie in my memory by concentrating on the few details I could recall and pulling the rest out of the great blur of forgetfulness— such has always been my method for bringing back the past.

The man had walked in the door wearing

white; with great difficulty I saw something in his hand—a wire cage. Bottles inside the cage. He must have been a milkman. The woman, with cupie-doll lips, opened up her dressing gown. He dropped his bottles. Then in the hurry of the ill-lit, flipping cards (I imagined it all still as if I were looking into the Mutascope), he tore her gown off in one jerk. His clothes and hers flew to the ground like settling birds. Then the man and women dropped to the floor, bodies moving in a spasm as the cards fell faster and faster, until the last one. When my film had run its course I didn't know what to do, my face hot and my nostrils wide to take in the erotic stink of the mildewing wood at the back of the attic.

118

Much later, with Peter, I still imagined sex as a pornographic movie. In hygiene class, the teacher told us that men had desires they couldn't control, and this had fit with my own fears. I thought that if he got too excited, Peter would turn into some person I didn't know, desperate to satisfy his needs, violent even. I thought that once the process began—his hand flying to my breast like metal to a magnet—nothing could stop it.

I loved to have him hold me as we sat in his car, stroking my hair and kissing me delicately. But if our kisses became too wide open and wet, I panicked—not unlike so many other women of my generation, back when virtue was something real that you could lose.

'No, we shouldn't,' I'd say, breaking away from him.

'Shh, *shush*, Frannie—don't get scared.' He'd rest his head on top of mine.

Gradually, my heart would slow and I'd say, 'I'm sorry, Peter.'

'It's all right. I understand.' We never discussed it more than that.

I didn't want passion because I was afraid of the speed, the way the cards tumbled down one after the other so fast you couldn't see any of the individual pictures. I didn't want it to be like that, a flash of moments. If sex was a Mutascope, I wanted to reach into the machine and take just one of those photographs, hold it in my hands, and stare at the grainy image of the man and the woman locked like Indian wrestlers. I wanted to see them frozen in that instant forever. I wanted passion to stop like a broken pocket-watch, a small circle of silver that I could hold safe in my hand forever.

119

Chapter Nine

FOUR DAYS LATER, we'd reached
New Mexico. I was driving, alive to the road as never
before. In that empty land, I became aware of every
bump, every turn, the bouncing and slipping of our
car. Sometimes the highway headed straight up into
the searing blue sky and then we'd pass between cliffs
that had been carved away to make the road. Yellow
signs would warn, CAUTION: CROSS WINDS, and our
little car would shift back and forth as if it could
barely contain itself.

In Texas, we'd driven by fields where the
harvested cotton was piled up in huge rectangles that
looked from a distance like trailer homes. Near the
fields, whole towns had been flecked with white, the
cotton clinging to the houses and lying thick on the
side of the road. Later, we'd passed pastureland,
rolling hills as beautiful as any in New Hampshire.
Then the land flattened and become brown. Now, we

skimmed through the pebbly desert, nothing big to see but occasional oil-pumping jacks. These machines, standing alone or in small clusters, looked like prehistoric birds, tirelessly bobbing their heads up and down to peck at something hidden, gleaming, just visible under the red dust.

A few days ago, Doris had called Annie and told her we might not visit Uncle Jack after all. We'd been thinking it would be more fun to see the Grand Canyon. Annie had been delighted with the idea. 'Keep Peggy for as long as you want, just so you get her back in time for school,' she'd said.

I had accepted this change of plans without arguing—without much thought, really. Of course we couldn't go to Uncle Jack's, not with Randy along. And to all of us, even me, the thought of dipping into the most humid part of Texas had begun to seem oppressive. We wanted the dry heat of the desert, all that emptiness and space.

Something in me had shifted during the last few days—I became dreamy and distracted. I felt almost like I did when I was thirteen, seduced by the beauty of the physical world. I enjoyed the tickle of my hair brushing my neck, admired Peg's green eyes between her freckled lids and Randy's pouted lips, and even loved the faint smell of coffee and perspiration that my own body gave off.

The rest of them seemed to feel it, too, for we had all settled into the lovely, heavy-limbed stupor of vacationers. The endless hours we spent in the car—during which our comfortable silences stretched longer and longer—soothed us. Time smoothed us, like a river wearing away rock.

121

As I drove us through the bright desert, I understood that my grief over my father, the fear of living without him, was finally lifting. I had become happy—more than happy, I was intoxicated.

I've always known my greatest joy after the ebbing of sorrow, like that summer we stayed at Aunt Katherine's. That was the first time we'd gone on vacation since our father came back from the war, from his war. The whole country, it seemed, was on vacation during those years. This was back when people took happiness seriously, planning picnics on red-checkered cloths, or embarking on gaudy trips into the wilderness with their fishing tackle and charcoal grills. Our vacation wasn't so carefree, though: Dad had been ordered by his doctor to take the summer off, for he still could not shake his deep depression.

The day we left for Aunt Katherine's, he had bought a yellow sailor's hat with a floppy brim. He wore it while he drove, and my mother scolded him good-naturedly, telling him he looked like a hobo. In fact, the hat seemed ridiculous on my father, otherwise so sober in his khakis and crisp white shirt. But he wore it like a bright flag signaling that he intended things to be better. He would be the father we remembered from before.

At some point—I was never sure whether it started during the war or after—our mother started to become nervous around Dad. She rarely spoke sharply to him or showed much affection, either. I think she was afraid that if he noticed her, if she became objectionable in any way, then he'd linger at work even later than he did every night, or perhaps

122

he'd vanish altogether. But as long as we were on vacation, Mom could relax. He had no warehouse to disappear to, no friends to stay with overnight (I believe he got dead drunk back then and fell asleep on peoples' couches). Some secret truce had been forged between my parents: he would be his old self again and she would too. I remember it was suddenly on that car trip that she began telling jokes, laughing with her mouth wide open, touching his hand, flirting.

Doris and I were able to yell and bicker without fear of upsetting them and I remember sitting in the back seat, screaming because she was playing with a tin car that I wanted. Finally it was given to me, and I held it in my palm before me and adored it. I don't know where that little car came from, whether it belonged to Doris or me, or what became of it, but I can picture it more vividly than any of them then— mother, father and Doris, whom I remember as blurry bodies.

The tin car had a key that went into a hole in its back bumper, and I could have wound it up and watched it bob along if there had been any floor to put it on. But I was perfectly happy to stare at it, examining the way the tin had been printed to look as if the car had windows and doors and people inside. Behind the light blue of the driver's window, you could see a man's head and his tiny hands clutching the top of a steering wheel. On the passenger window was a silhouette of a woman's head in a kerchief. And if you looked at the car head on, you saw their faces superimposed on the windshield. With its bright paint in the pink cup of my palm, that tin car seemed like a

123

bit of my family's happiness frozen into a model, a monument.

Yet I remember puzzling over the car, too. Several things disturbed me: for example, the back seat was empty. Where were Doris and I? And worse was the troubling vertigo of the perspective. If I looked at the car from an angle, I could see the front of the man's face and his silhouette in the side window, both at once. Peering through the windshield, the man looked rather clownish, but from the side, he seemed intent and preoccupied. The man was two men at the same time, or perhaps I was two girls looking at him from different angles. For all the joy the tin car gave me, this inaccuracy seemed to hint that what I held in my hand, what seemed solid and real, was far beyond my comprehension.

Now, as I drove, I thought of Dad. Only recently, I'd begun to admit to myself a suspicion I'd always had. My father might have had lovers. I had found no inexplicable letters, no photographs of strange women, among his things after he died. I had no hard evidence, just memories that didn't add up— the labored politeness between my parents, my mother watching him so hungrily, the way she apologized to us for his absences, over-hasty to make excuses. Even in that drive to Aunt Katherine's, I see something suspicious. My mother's happiness—the openness of her face when she laughed—suggested some private struggle from which she had temporarily been released, some hidden world within her.

WE STOPPED IN Albuquerque that afternoon because Peggy wanted to look at the stores.

All I wanted was to get out of the heat. 'Just drop me off at a motel. I don't care which one, as long as it has a swimming pool,' I said. 'I'm dying to take a dip and lie around in the air conditioning.'

To my surprise, Randy decided to stay with me. 'I feel carsick,' he said. 'I'll hang out and read for a while.'

They left us at a Holiday Inn. Randy and I padded through the silent, musty hallways to our rooms. At the door, I handed him his key. 'Why don't you sit out by the pool?'

'OK,' he said, shyly.

As I swam laps, he lay in a lounge chair, reading a thick book. I glanced at him occasionally, worried that perhaps I should be more friendly, but he seemed content. After I'd had my shower, gotten dressed again, and puttered around my room for a while, I strolled back to the pool and found him still intent on his book. I sat down beside him. He wore swim trucks and an unbuttoned shirt that revealed a slice of his smooth, tan chest.

'You didn't even go in,' I said.

He looked up. 'Oh, I forgot. It's just that I haven't had a chance to read in a while and I'm really into this book.'

'Oh? What are you reading?' I craned my neck so I could see the cover.

'Marcuse. My brother—he's a junior in college—he lent me this book. He told me that if I want to major in sociology, which I do, this is what I should read.'

'Hmm,' I said, pulling up a lounge chair. 'So what's it about?'

125

'Well, it's about how the people in power use all these tactics to make us conform—like religion. But if that social control stops working, or falls apart, then more and more people drop out of society. Marcuse is sort of a Marxist, but he argues that maybe revolution isn't necessary for change, because if enough people become alienated from society, then the society won't work.'

'Well, that sounds plausible,' I said. 'Do you think that applies to Vietnam? Do you think the war would end if enough men refused to fight?'

'That's so weird,' he said. 'That's what I was thinking about as I was reading.'

'My father was a conscientious objector during World War II.'

'Really?' Randy's eyes got wide and he began asking me about Dad. As we talked, I was aware of the motel around us, the smell of the chlorine from the pool and the stuffy atrium in which we sat. It was strange, almost sinful, to be at a motel in the afternoon, a place abandoned by everyone but illicit lovers.

'Aren't you hungry?' I asked.

He smiled and nodded.

'Well, I'll treat you.'

We sat at a booth in the coffee shop and ordered sandwiches. 'You know,' I said, when my egg salad came, 'I've been thinking. It's strange that you and Peg get along so well. She's not at all interested in books or ideas. She lacks that quiet side you have.'

He looked up from his food, caught off-guard, then smiled in his own shy way. 'Well, we don't always get along so great. But I never think of it like that anyway, I mean, Peg not having something I do. I always thought it was the other way around.' He looked out the window, at the burnt grass of the motel's front lawn and the parking lot where the cars shone. 'You should just see her in school. Everyone's crazy about her.'

'How did you two meet?' It was not like me to ask personal questions—usually they seemed rude. But with Randy, I felt a sort of intimacy after all those hours in the car.

He took a bite, washed it down. 'Well, I barely knew her when, one day, she comes up and grabs my arm and then we're running around on the football field laughing our guts out. Then she says, "Hey, let's have some ice cream," and so we go to the Baskin-Robbins and sit there talking for a long time. But even though I didn't know her, it didn't seem awkward or anything.'

'You mean you couldn't get a word in edgewise.'

'Yeah,' he laughed.

The waitress passed by and Randy ordered another Coke. After she left I asked, 'Why did Peg run up to you that day? Did she ever tell you?'

'I guess I never thought to ask,' he laughed again and swiped his hair out of his eyes. 'If I did ask her, she'd probably say, "I just did it, that's all." She says I think too hard.'

'Well,' I said, feeling suddenly shy, 'maybe she saw there was something to you. Peg's a very bright girl.'

I suppose I embarrassed him. His eyes

127

darted toward mine and then away. 'I don't know,' he said. 'I still have no idea why she likes me. I think she gets bored with me sometimes.'

'Now, Randy, you know how much she cares for you. She can barely stand to be away from you. Today, for instance—she didn't want to let you out of her sight. She kept begging you to go shopping with her. You'd think she would have had enough, after all that time in the car.'

He laughed, 'Yeah, she gets pretty worked up sometimes. But, you know, it's because I'm going to college soon.' He picked at his potato chips reflectively. 'After that, forget it. This is, like, our last time to really be together. Once I'm gone, I bet she'll forget about me. That's what kills me.'

128

I knew he was right about Peg. I could imagine her throwing an operatic scene as he left, wailing and clinging to him. But a month later, she might tap another boy on the shoulder.

'Randy,' I said, 'if the person's not right, or the time's not right, it's important to let go. That's what I've learned anyway. It's better to let go than to hang on too long.'

'Is that why you never got married?' he asked. Then he looked sheepish. 'I'm sorry, I guess that wasn't such a cool thing to say.'

'No, it's all right.' And I found myself telling him about Peter's letter, about our failed courtship. 'He's the only man I've been serious about, really,' I said. 'Peter and my family and our town, that's all I've known. But now that I'm out here it all seems so far away. I miss it very much.' I paused for a moment, picturing the cold river that cut through our town, past the black brick of the factory buildings. 'It's all so wonderfully old. I love that.'

'But you're glad to be away, aren't you?' Randy was leaning forward, intent, forgetting to finish his sandwich.

'Being out here has changed things. I always thought of my life as set in stone, as if someone else had already made all the decisions for me—I thought I'd stay in our house until I grew old, just live a quiet life. So when Doris wanted to go on this trip, she had a hard time getting me out of New Hampshire. Now, things are different. I love that town, but from a long way off.'

'Well,' Randy said. He took a bite of his sandwich and chewed, not knowing what to say. 'I guess I can relate to that, because I'm leaving home soon. I think college'll be OK, but I'm going to miss all my friends.'

'The thing is,' I was gathering steam, beginning to understand myself, 'I love that house, but I can't quite go back to it yet. Seeing my father's old room, hearing the hallway creak like it always did, I think I'd just get depressed all over again. And with Peter . . . well, I don't have the strength to plunge into that again, either. Not yet. My favorite thing right now is to think about Peter and our town and my wonderful house, to treasure those things from far away, like the dearest memories.'

'But you are going to get back together with him, aren't you?' Randy had a worried look on his face.

I laughed. 'We'll see. It will all sort itself out, I'm sure.'

129

'Nothing sorts itself out,' Randy said with a dead sound in his voice. 'Things just get more complicated.' He gazed out the window, silent for a moment. Then he glanced back at me and said quietly, 'At the beginning of this summer, I was thinking about deferring—you know, starting college next year. I wanted to stay with Peg. She meant that much to me. But lately, sometimes it's so obvious we have nothing in common. I mean, when I try to talk to her seriously, it's like she doesn't get it at all. Still, it kills me that I have to leave her. Maybe if I stayed we could work it out eventually.'

'Oh, Randy, I really don't think you should put off college.'

He sighed, looked down. 'Well, it's not like I have a choice. I've got to go. I'm almost eighteen. If I don't go, I'll get drafted.' His voice cracked. 'Even being *in* college, I could get drafted.'

'That's right,' I said. 'I'd forgotten about that. Oh, what a terrible thing you have to face.'

'Yeah, it's like a bad dream. My cousin got drafted, and now he's over there.' Randy looked almost like he wanted to cry—I don't think I'd ever seen a man so vulnerable, so open to me.

'Don't worry,' I said firmly, 'Whatever happens, you won't go. There are ways to get out. I promise you.'

And then, for a moment, all the wars of my life seemed like one long war. Not even a war exactly, but just something that sucked men away. No matter how tightly you held onto them, it always pried them out of your arms, whisked them away, and you were left with nothing but their shirt stays and their razor blades bleeding rust and their cracked buttons. If you were lucky, a faint smell lingered, too, though that slowly faded. What was Vietnam but a name for something else, that age-old power that takes our men away and makes spinsters of us all?

THAT EVENING, PEG and Doris came back in a wonderful, giddy mood.

'This place is such a hick town!' Peg said. 'They had the dumbest stores. But we did have fun at the rifle range.'

And she and Doris looked at each other and burst out laughing, quite pleased with themselves. Apparently, Peg knew how to shoot a bit, so they'd rented rifles and fired off rounds at targets under the hot sun all day.

'Let's go to a steak house for dinner,' Doris said. She seemed to be in a celebratory mood. 'Is everyone as hungry as I am?'

'Actually, I'm not very hungry, but I think it would be fun,' I said.

'I'm hungry,' Randy said. 'I'm always hungry.' Neither he nor I mentioned our late-afternoon lunch together. It was as if we both recognized that something improper, maybe even shameful, had happened.

Doris drove to the restaurant, and we sat at a table where we could look out a huge picture window. Over a strip of gas stations and warehouses and neon signs, the sky glowed pink and orange before it finally faded into deep blue. Doris and I drank a bottle of wine between us, which was altogether too much. When it was time to leave, she

131

handed Randy the keys and said, 'We're smashed. You drive home.'

Once we got back to the motel, I collapsed on top of my bed, feeling the cheap chintz bedspread crinkle under my skin, and enjoying the lovely exhaustion of my limbs. 'You should have gone swimming, Doris. I feel so relaxed.'

'I think that's the wine.' She sat on her own bed and began to sew up a small rip in her dress.

'Doris,' I said in a hazy, far-away voice, 'I've been thinking. Do you suppose Dad ever cheated on Mom?'

'What!' her head bobbed up, eyes fixed on me. I hadn't expected her to be so shocked. 'Frannie! What's gotten into you?'

'Oh, I don't know,' I said dreamily. The wine made me feel like I was studying the subject from a long way off. 'Lately, I've just been trying to figure out why things seemed so strange between them. I don't mean anything specific, really. It's just that he became so distant and she . . . well, she always reminded me of a girl who's been stood up.'

Doris held the needle and dress poised in her hands. She'd forgotten about her sewing. 'I'm surprised that you brought it up, but I do know what you're talking about. He was so removed, those last few years with her. And he certainly went away often enough, didn't he? Where was it he went?'

'I don't know. Business.'

'Hmmm,' Doris looked down, went back to sewing. 'There *was* something funny about it—but I never thought it had anything to do with a woman. He just got kind of batty after the war. Couldn't really be close to anyone. He was like that with us, too, don't you think? I mean, he was always very kind and sweet, but you got the sense that his thoughts were somewhere else.'

'But Mom . . . '

Doris looked down at her sewing. 'Yes, well, she just couldn't take it—that's what I always thought. I mean, she was so nervous anyway.'

'Yes, she worried about everything.' I said this fondly, for I remembered her panicked hug as I stepped out the door to walk to school, her anxious questions about mittens and homework assignments and lunch pails when I came home.

'The thing is,' Doris said, 'he didn't want to be with her. I always thought it was because she depended on him for so much. Remember when we were very little? It was always, "Your mother can't be disturbed. You mustn't bother her." He treated her like an invalid. When he had his breakdown, she was probably no help at all. Then he started avoiding her, that whole thing. You'd think they would have patched it up later. I guess they never did. They pretended to get on perfectly, but they always had their own secret war going.'

'We'll never know about that war, will we?'

'No,' she said.

I sat up in my bed. Doris, under the bedside lamp, looked girlish, the light curving along her cheek and pooling in the hollow of her collarbone. I felt as if we were in our old bedroom, as if we were still girls. Oh, those awful months after our mother died, the two of us curled in our twin beds with the light on; we could lie there for hours at a time, silent, as if our

133

beds were coffins. We'd had an understanding then. We hadn't needed to speak about it—what we thought about her death.

It is the obvious that fades away with time. Until this moment I had forgotten the simple truth about our mother, or what had seemed like the simple truth way back then. I started speaking slowly, as if from a long way off, the way off of our girlhood. 'What I wonder,' I said, 'is why Mom was out walking in the middle of the night on that road. She never went for walks. Why would she just go out one night like that and get killed?'

Doris gazed straight at me. 'We both know why. Everyone was too polite to say it, but we always knew why, didn't we?'

'Do you really think it was that? That she did it on purpose?'

'I saw her when she ran out of the house. But you know that,' Doris said calmly, smoothing out the skirt she'd been sewing. 'She was in one of those moods. Her voice was all shaky and strange. Hysterical, I guess it's properly called. She put on that coat like she couldn't feel it, the way she stabbed her hands into the sleeves. She told me she wanted air.'

'Yes,' I said. 'I can picture all that. She was like that. But do you think she did it on purpose, Doris?'

'Maybe somewhere in the back of her mind she knew what was going to happen that night. But who can say? The fact was, she had deep problems, and for whatever reason, Dad didn't concern himself with it. I don't think he understood how sick she was.'

'You think she was mentally ill?'

'Yes, in a way,' Doris sighed. 'She managed to seem all right most of the time.'

'I wish we had asked Dad about her, after she died—I mean *really* asked him.'

'He wouldn't have been able to tell us anything,' Doris said. 'He always believed her death was an accident. He was like that, Frannie.'

'You know,' I said, 'even after he got better, we always thought of him as the sick one. But really it was Mom, wasn't it?'

'Yes,' she said. 'We pretended things were one way, but all along, they were another way, the opposite almost.'

We fell silent, both brooding. I was remembering myself as a little girl, how I struggled to write consoling letters to my father when he was in that hospital, drinking the sea water. 'Don't worry, we are well,' I'd slowly draft in my best penmanship, and sign my letter, 'With deepest regards, your loving daughter, Frannie.' The way my mother taught me.

When I finished, I'd give the letter to her, and she'd address it and let me lick the stamp. 'Oh, what a good girl you are!' she'd say. 'What a good girl,' she'd repeat absently, as if the words had lost their meaning or become a code for something else.

It's the most obvious things you forget; you forget the atmosphere that people carry around them like a smell. My mother smelled of mint and cigarette smoke, the scent of camphor mixed with the musk of death. She'd lean over a pot on the stove, the steam around her face like a veil: 'It's not going to work. I've spoiled it. Oh dear, I've spoiled it.' Her voice rose into a wavering wail on the most innocent

135

sentences. You couldn't help but feel her panic when you were around her, that terror over teapots and burnt toast.

'You know Doris, at some level I always thought it was my fault. But now I don't feel that way anymore. *Whooshh*.' I made a sweeping movement with my hand. 'Gone.'

She laughed. 'Oh it's never gone, silly girl.'

'But it *is* gone. I loved it really, is what I have to admit to you now. Taking care of her—that's what I loved. "Mom, you forgot your car keys." "Oh yes, thank you dear. What would I do without you, Frannie?" I loved worrying about Mom and Dad that way, believing I was the one who could save them. I always thought it was up to me, you know?'

Doris smiled and smacked her pack of Kools to work out the first cigarette. It came out in stages, longer with each smack. 'But now you're at loose ends, huh?'

'Loose ends,' I said. 'I'm all loose ends. I don't know what I should do with myself. What should I do with myself?'

'Have fun.' She laughed, sticking the cigarette in her mouth so it wagged on her lips.

Have fun, I thought to myself. That was what my mother used to call after us, tentatively, as we ran out to play. 'Have fun!' she'd say, pecking Doris on the cheek when a boy's car pulled up in front of our house. And as my mother went off to her bridge group, my father would call, absent-mindedly from behind a book, 'Have fun, dear.' We were a family constantly wishing fun on one another. But what was fun? Fun was finally shaking off that weight of worry, the atmosphere of contained hysteria, that so often fogged our house.

What were my parents' deaths? Hiroshima and Nagasaki, two bombs that blasted me. The Japs wouldn't surrender after the first one, so we had to drop the other one on them. And after the second one, they learned. They learned how to give up.

Chapter Ten

THE NEXT DAY, we planned to push on to Flagstaff. Doris drove for several hours. Finally she declared, 'I'm starting to see double. I can't do this anymore.'

'I'll drive,' Peg piped up from the back seat. 'I'm good at it.'

The highway ran into Arizona as straight as a needle, desolate and windswept. 'Well,' Doris said, 'there's nothing to hit around here anyway, so you might as well get your practice.' She slowed the car and pulled over. 'I'll sit up front with you.'

Peg turned out to be a good driver, just as she'd promised, or rather, not so much good as dedicated—she leaned over the wheel in deep concentration.

I sat in the back with Randy, who was trying to do a crossword puzzle. After a while he lay the paper on his lap. 'Uggh,' he said, letting his head loll against the seat, 'I can't do this. I get so dizzy.'

'Here.' I took the paper. 'I'll read the questions to you for a while.' I read the clues out loud and everyone shouted answers—we all welcomed this frenzy of activity after so many hours of the drowsy stupor that had come over us.

When we'd almost finished the puzzle, I dropped my pen and it rolled into the crack of the seat. 'Darn!' I said. 'Darn, darn.' I ran my hand along the fold of vinyl. 'Randy, can you help me?'

'Don't worry about it. I've got another one.' He reached up and produced a pen from behind his ear.

'Thanks,' I said, taking it. I stared down at the puzzle again, trying not to think about what I held, how it had just been nestled in the wispy, curling hair over his ear. I tried not to think about his tanned temple, a soft place where one could lay a hand and feel his heartbeat. I tried not to think about these things, but the pen was still warm and I couldn't help imagining (when I tapped it against my cheek) that it smelled the same way he did, an earthy scent of sweat and crushed grass.

At dusk, we traveled higher into the mountains and tasted crisp air that reminded me of New Hampshire, a tingle in my mouth like soda water. Our headlights swept before us, illuminating the tall grass so it looked unearthly, sticks of wire or bristles of a giant hairbrush. The sky took a long time to fade, disappearing in a pink-purple blush behind the mountains ahead of us. Though cars sometimes passed us

139

with a swish, it seemed as if we were the only people in the world.

Doris switched on the radio, and we listened to the news from Chicago, where the Democrats were holding their convention. Much talk about Humphrey and McGovern and—our favorite—McCarthy. Then the newscaster's voice got low, the way newscasters do when they're called on to act concerned. 'Unfortunately, violence has broken out in the streets of Chicago,' he said, and we turned up the volume.

The antiwar protestors had thrown rocks and jeered at the police. I certainly didn't condone that. But the police had responded in a way that seemed just plain crazy. They'd lobbed tear gas at the crowd—some people heard them chanting 'kill, kill, kill'—and chased young people through the streets, beating them to the ground. They'd even attacked newsmen.

When the Chicago police chief came on with his statement—law and order, keeping the peace—Doris couldn't stand any more and snapped off the radio.

'If they want to keep the peace so badly, why don't they end the goddamn war?' she said.

'It's terrible,' I clucked. 'All this talk about Bobby Kennedy, how much he meant to the Democratic party. Why, if he was still alive, he'd be out there marching in the streets.'

Peg, next to me in the back seat, laughed. 'You all are great. I wish we were there together, right now, fighting the cops. You two would hit them over their heads with your purses.'

'Darn right we would,' I said.

The kids didn't seem as upset as we were. 'It doesn't make me mad, it just makes me depressed,' Randy said in a quiet voice. 'It's so predictable. They're putting up chain-link fences around the convention hall, as if that way no one will have to think about the war. What do you want to bet Humphrey doesn't even mention Vietnam once?' Randy had been reading the papers every day, and the rest of us, whose minds had grown vacation-fuzzy, depended on him for our news.

We talked about politics until our voices got tired, and finally we fell silent, each in our own dreamy world, drugged by the motion of the car. After a while, I fell into a pleasant lassitude—which became an unwillingness to stand up when we pulled over at a rest stop. When I did get out to walk around the Stuckey's, everything seemed unreal, as in a dream. Near the register, I saw a huge display of lollypops and t-shirts and souvenir glasses and stickers. I had become so dazed that I craved everything on these racks. I stared at strangers, too, those other travelers who shuffled around in the yellowish light. They looked half asleep, with their shirts untucked and their shoes untied, just emerged from the cocoon of their cars.

141

It wasn't only the hours upon hours of being cooped up in the car that made me feel strange. Something else had happened. Randy drove the last stretch of road into Flagstaff, and I sat behind him, watching. In the dark, I could just make out the tendrils of hair on his nape, the bump of bone that stood out above the neck of his t-shirt, the dark skin that would be so smooth, if only I could touch it.

Did it seem wrong to crave him like that? I did feel a stab of guilt when I glanced over at Peg, who sat beside him on the front seat; she was watching him drive like she couldn't get enough. But no, I didn't feel guilty, not really—after all, I didn't want to take Randy from her. I only wanted to look.

I wanted to look because for years I hadn't paid much attention to men, hadn't been interested, and now all of a sudden I was. I liked to imagine the teasing touch of a man's fingers on my face. Not Randy's fingers, really. Maybe Peter's. I knew what would happen when I saw Peter again: he'd stare at me with those whiskey-colored eyes. 'I've missed you so much,' he'd groan. And then I'd be lost. I'd be his Frannie, his.

142

Oh Lord, it had been so long since I had let any man get to me. After Peter left, I had cultivated an inner blankness, a calm. Of course I noticed men, but I had no appetite for them, so to speak. Why should I have, when I imagined that no man would ever love me? And so I had dedicated myself to other things besides love, things that can fill up a life just as easily: the revelation of steaming teapots and fresh-starched sheets and light playing across a red vase. I tried to experience each pleasure separately, to ration out these small joys to myself like the chocolates in the box I kept on a high shelf and only took down when company came.

But now I was ready to live willy-nilly, to go home and give myself up to Peter. I wanted to meet him under compromising and unseemly circumstances—at a motel, in the dark of my own bedroom, down by the river. I wanted to eat that box of chocolates all at once, until I made myself sick with satisfaction: the marischino cherry coated in goo; dark chocolates as strong as coffee, caramel that makes your throat ache with sweetness.

AT ABOUT NINE o'clock we pulled into Flagstaff and found a motel. After Doris and I had thrown our suitcases on the beds and washed our faces, I said to her, 'Give me your change. I'm going to call him.'

'Why do you need change?' she said. 'You can call from our room. I'll go out and have a cigarette.'

'No, that's all right. I want to use a pay-phone. I don't know why, but I'd feel embarrassed here.'

She emptied her pocketbook on the bureau. 'OK, have it your way. Here's some dimes. Oh and wait—here's something else. Some perfume.' She picked out a tiny, ruby-colored bottle. 'Roses,' she said. 'Put it on.'

'What do you mean? He can't smell through the telephone.'

'No—but you'll feel more . . . I don't know, girlish? Don't you think?'

'I suppose it's worth a try,' I said and touched some to my neck.

'Oh my,' she said, as she watched me dab, and I heard the ache in her voice. 'I wish it was me.'

In a heady daze, I stepped outside into a small-town night that smelled of cedar trees and diesel. Our motel sat on what I assumed was Flagstaff's main street, a two-laner lined with little stores, all closed for the night. As I passed each low build-ing—Elks club, donut place, library, notions shop, and an elementary school that no doubt was decorated inside with children's painted pine cones—I was reminded of my own town.

I pretended then that Peter walked silently by my side. We used to stroll along at night through town sometimes, gazing into the dark windows of stores. For a moment or two I fooled myself and felt him beside me, imagined myself turning to see the glimmering whiteness of his face and his look of shy affection. But it was only me—only me playing a game with myself.

I found a phone booth near the park, nestled between a water fountain and a few trees. I sat down, arranging my skirt under me and running a hand over my hair. At the same time, I wanted to laugh at my silliness—so nervous, so convinced he would be able to see me. I lifted the phone from the hook, felt a pang in my stomach, put it back.

The booth had begun to fill with the flow-ery, sweet-and-sour smell of Doris's perfume. Under-neath the phone was a wooden shelf with graffiti etched into it: TONI 'N' TIM, BULLDOGS FOREVER, I LUV DANNY, GO TO HELL, GAIL P. I felt a strange sort of kinship with all the other people who had sat here, afraid to call someone, or aching to, who had taken out their penknives and scratched their passion into the wood. I ran my thumbnail over its surface, making a thin mark. What would I have written, if I dared? My passion had no name nor any face, not even Peter's really. Perhaps I would have scratched out, I'M IN A TIZZY—that would have been the only way to

144

describe this buzzing in me, as if suddenly the electricity had been snapped on.

After sitting there a long time, I finally dialed his number, all in a rush. As I waited, my heart beat in my ears, the phone began ringing—and went on ringing. After a minute or two, I realized he wasn't there, and hung up with a certain relief. My hands were so sweaty that I had to wipe them on my skirt. How must I have looked then, a woman lit up by the wavering fluorescence of a phonebooth, as if on stage—a woman sitting in a glass box, all alone in an empty park?

As I opened the door (that particular, bellows-like squack as it folded in two) and stepped outside, I felt a rush of disappointment. I had needed so desperately to hear Peter's voice, to prove to myself he was still out there, waiting. The truth was, I was afraid. What if he had gone back to Eva? What if he'd only imagined he loved me? What if I never felt this dangerous happiness again?

I strolled along listening to the crickets and the crackle of an electric line overhead; suddenly it occurred to me that my happiness did not depend on Peter. If I had to, I could get along without him, as I always had—I could find other things to love. For instance, I loved being out west; even the words gave me a thrill, the hot desert air of it, the freedom.

As I neared our motel, I suddenly caught a whiff of some fragrance, and I looked around for a blossoming tree or a patch of flowers. But there was nothing to give off any odor—only clipped grass and a near-empty parking lot. Then I realized that the mysterious scent came from me. It was Doris's rose perfume, wafting off my own skin.

IT DIDN'T TAKE long to drive to the Grand Canyon the next morning, and we soon found ourselves hiking through a hushed forest toward the rim. The day was perfect—a bright blue sky and a light breeze. We spent an hour or so taking pictures, scrambling out onto ledges to look down, reading the signs, before Doris disappeared into the visitors' center and came back with a map.

She unfurled it before me. 'Let's hike a few miles down. Don't you think the kids would love that?'

'You mean on mules?'

'No,' she laughed. 'On our own two feet, silly. I don't want to be like those fat, lazy tourists.'

'You know how I hate hiking,' I said. 'Leave me here. I won't mind at all.'

'No, Frannie, you must.'

'Really, I'm in the mood to just sit in the sun. I'll have a fine time. Don't worry.'

Doris snorted, her version of a sarcastic laugh. 'You're worse than the fat tourists. Well, you do whatever you want. I'll go find the kids.' And so, equipped with a cheap canteen and some sandwiches, they all set off on the steep path that wound to the bottom of the canyon.

I wandered around until I spied a little outcropping of stone far from the crowded overlooks and sheltered by twisted trees. I sat hugging my knees and staring out at the view, but no matter how I concentrated, I couldn't make the Grand Canyon real.

Instead, it seemed like a stage set that hung a few feet away from me, flat and fake as a picture postcard. I sat, waiting to be awed by the majesty of nature or somesuch thing, but I just wasn't capable. Instead, I could only feel my own lack of feeling, the smallness of my own imagination.

It had been the same with my mother's death. At the time, I had been disturbed by how little I reacted. I didn't cry at her funeral. I didn't stop eating or sleeping. Instead, I looked after my grieving, guilty father—cooking for him when the casseroles stopped arriving, ironing his shirts for work. At the time, I convinced myself I had to bury my feelings and act cheerful, so I could properly care for Dad and Doris. But to tell the truth, for months I could not bring myself to believe in her death.

147

At first, I pretended she'd gotten held up at the market and would be back soon. The house had an expectant air, as if any moment she'd waltz in, the grocery bags making their particular rattling, crinkling sound in her arms—as if any moment she'd call in that hesitant voice, 'Girls? Frances? Doris?' Later, I imagined she'd gone to stay with relatives. Little by little, I ceased to listen for her step on the stair or to expect her smell of mint to issue up from the sofa.

Then one day, I can't say when exactly, her death became a fact. Instead of thinking of her all the time, I tried not to think of her at all—she had become an achy, tender spot I wanted to leave alone so it could heal. But she appeared to me in dreams, sitting in another room while we had dinner, or looking in at me through a window. In my sleep, I was always making excuses for our behavior, the way we snubbed her. 'We'd invite you in if we could, but we don't have any room,' I'd say to her.

Slowly, without noticing, I had begun to believe my father's story: she had been out for a walk, that was all. It was the driver's fault; the car had sped around the corner, too fast for her (she was standing in the middle of a hairpin curve on Hillandale Way), no time for her to run, no time for anything but her white face turning, the O of her mouth.

Hillandale Way—for years, just the name of that road made me want to retch. After Mom died, they widened the dangerous part, where the road curved around a mossy cliff, and put in some signs— or so I heard, anyway. Even before Mother, that kink in the road had a reputation. Once there had been head-on; another time, a dog killed. She must have known about the dog.

Still, even now, I believed her death was an accident, though not the kind I imagined as a girl. Not the speeding car, reckless as it rounded a bend in the dark road. Not the screaming woman, lit up in her last moment, not that kind of accident. Hers was an accident of feeling, a whim that went too far—a woman with her coat half on, running out the door, frantic for release. If she could have undone it the next day, I know she would have.

I SAT FOR hours in my spot, staring out at the purples and pinks of the canyon walls, at the birds that glided below me. And then the shrubs behind me began rustling. I suppose I started, jerking my head toward the sound, though even before I saw who it was, I knew—Randy. He stepped out of the bushes, ducking under a tree branch, and then stood before me. 'Hi,' he said, almost whispered.

I jumped up, straightening my skirt. 'What happened to Doris and Peg? Are they all right?'

'Oh, yeah, they're fine. They're still walking down into the canyon.' He ran his fingers through his long forelock of hair and tossed his head back.

'Well, what happened?' I felt my face squint up the way it did when I was confused.

'It was awful,' he said. 'Peg and I started screaming at each other, and then Doris said we were giving her a headache and told us to shut up. Well, I knew we couldn't shut up, so I said I'd go back up to the top and wait for them. I didn't want to ruin everything.'

'Whatever could have made you two fight like that?' I said this warily: I wasn't sure he wanted me to ask that.

He seemed glad I did, though. 'It's so stupid. Peg started throwing twigs and pebbles at me and saying stuff like, "Stop staring into space, you jerk." She always wants me to pay attention to her, but I just didn't have the energy right then. We hadn't been getting along since last night, and I didn't feel like talking—I just wanted to think, you know? But she was getting mad because I wouldn't keep up this dumb, jokey conversation with her. That's when she started throwing stuff. So I said, "Stop it, Peg. I'm getting really, really angry." Of course, that only made her throw more stuff at me. So I grabbed her arm and twisted it—not that hard, I swear—and she started screaming at me. We were screaming like little kids, like we couldn't even think anymore.' He seemed to have finished his story, his hands hanging limp at his sides. But then he added, 'It was awful,' and looked away.

'Oh dear,' I said. 'Well, I'm sure you'll make up with her. After all, you two have been stuck in a car for days. That tends to make people bicker.'

'I know,' he said, his voice cracking. 'But it's much worse than that. It's not just like we're getting on each others' nerves. At this point, I think we hate each other.'

'I'm sorry,' I said, and reached out tentatively to pat his shoulder. Perhaps he thought I was going to hug him—as I put my hand out, he more or less fell against me, his arms circling my waist. I could feel his body heaving. He wasn't exactly crying, but he breathed raggedly, as if he wanted to sob.

'Now, now,' I said, awkwardly stroking his back. 'Now, now. It's all right.'

He shifted in my arms so his cheek brushed against mine. Still, I couldn't see his face. 'Frannie,' he whispered. 'The worst part, the thing that makes me feel guilty whenever I'm around Peg, is that I can't stop thinking about you.'

'What?' I struggled out of his arms, stepped away. 'You musn't say that.' The back of my neck prickled, as if all my fear sat there.

He looked scared, too, his mouth clamped tight like he was waiting to be hit. 'I'm sorry. Never mind.'

I looked down and noticed how dirty my toes had gotten in the sandles I wore. I didn't want to look up at him, but I made myself do it. 'It's all right,' I said. 'It's really, really all right.' My perception had become strange—we seemed to be frozen together in this one moment, stuck on the verge of something. Time lengthened out the way it does when you stand on a high diving board, feeling it shiver underneath you just before you plunge off. And then I heard myself say, 'I think about you, too.'

He stepped close, touched my shoulder. 'I want to be with you,' he said. 'Maybe when I get to college, we could meet. I just want . . . ' Then he leaned over as if to sniff me. Gently, he kissed my lips. His mouth settled on mine as delicately as I might dab a napkin there.

I pulled back. 'Randy, you know this is impossible.' My voice sounded hoarse, strange.

'I know,' he said, touching my face. Oh what a tender boy. I hadn't realized how much I craved that, the girlish pout of his lips and the way he cupped my cheek and chin in one hand.

'This can't happen,' I said. 'I'm ashamed I let it get this far. You know I care for you,' I heard my voice break when I said this. 'But we must behave ourselves. Let's just try to get through the rest of the trip without doing anything we'll regret. Let's stop it now, Randy.'

He leaned in close, slid his arms around my waist, and I felt his breath on my face with its particular smell—dried sweat and dust and grape chewing gum. 'I've never felt like this before. I've always been scared of girls, even Peg. Not you, though.'

'Yes,' I said, and gently pushed him away. 'I know how you feel. But we have to stop.'

'I can't. I just can't,' he said, his voice

becoming high. Suddenly I was struck by how young he was. His eyes—when I glimpsed them behind the white reflections on his glasses—were steady and intent, not a bit of guile in them. 'Look,' he said. 'I'll take a bus back tonight. Things aren't working out with Peg anyway. And then when I get to college, we'll meet . . . '

'No,' I said. 'Impossible.'

He turned away. 'Why? You don't really care about me, do you?'

'Yes, I do—very much. But please, please understand.'

'What do I need to understand?' Here he hugged his own chest, as if he'd suddenly taken a chill. 'If you felt like I do, you wouldn't care about anything else. You'd just want to be with me.'

'I don't want to hurt anyone, Randy,' I said sternly.

He'd turned toward the canyon. I couldn't see his face, but his voice was flat, dead. 'If I go home tonight, and then call you and we meet later, Peg will never know.'

'It's not her—it's you. You're almost half my age. I don't want to hurt you.'

'Well, you are.' He turned toward me, and I saw he had been crying. I had never seen a man so weak. What could I do but step toward him—one dizzy step like walking a tightrope—and hold him? He nuzzled my face, and then kissed me, his tongue curling inside my mouth like it belonged there.

And oh, I kissed him back, twining my arms around him and feeling the sweaty warmth of his skin through his t-shirt. I slipped one hand under the shirt

152

and touched the slickness of his back, the way the muscles and bone slithered under his skin with their own intelligence. His lips trailed down my neck and made me shudder. Nothing had ever felt so good.

'You can call me someday.' I said in a rough, strange voice. 'But we can't do this now.' Oh Lord, I was so close to tears at the unfairness of it. How Doris always got the boys, how they always flocked to her. And now here he was, a teenage boy to make up for all the ones I never got, and I couldn't have him. 'I wish you had come along when I was eighteen. I wanted so badly to meet a boy like you, but there never were any. None of them ever understood me.'

'I know,' he said soothingly, running a finger down my cheek. 'I know. I would have loved you so much.'

'But now,' I said, pulling away, 'we have to go find Peg. You need to make up with her. And then we have to pretend none of this happened. Can you do that?'

'Yes,' he said. 'It'll be fine, Frannie. We'll figure something out.'

'All right,' I said, and purposefully waded into the bushes and out onto the path. Randy followed, and we walked through the woods until we came to the gift shops and historic markers and the little bands of tourists. We didn't say anything, didn't touch, but an understanding had arisen between us. Together, we started down the path into the canyon, puffs of red dust rising under our feet. We moved fast, our arms swinging, and a few times our hands touched, as if by accident.

153

After fifteen minutes or so, we saw Peg and Doris heading up the trail toward us. They waved, and when we got close, Peg ran up and hugged Randy. 'Please don't be mad anymore, *please*.' Her red hair spilled down her back as she gazed up at him; her eyes became slits in her crumpled face.

'I won't,' he said, holding her and rocking her.

I couldn't watch. I continued down the trail to Doris. 'Look what I found,' I said. 'I thought I'd bring him back.' I was surprised at how calm, how normal, my voice sounded.

Doris dropped her bag to the ground and sighed. 'I know, I know. I'll admit it's a mess. All right, so it wasn't the greatest idea to bring him along. But don't gloat Frannie, just don't gloat, OK?'

'Oh Doris, I wasn't going to gloat. I'm glad he came along. It's just—we're all cranky and feeling funny today. Don't you think?'

'No, it's more. I'm beginning to see how right you were,' she lowered her voice. 'I've been letting Peg get away with murder. I never should have let her talk me into taking him.'

'Oh, don't worry, Doris,' I patted her arm. 'It'll all work out for the best.'

THAT NIGHT, WE had dinner at a pizza place. Peg sat wedged against Randy on their side of the booth. He and I avoided each other's eyes, though I never once felt our connection had been broken. She curled up against his arm and chattered at him: 'Hey, you want a sip of my Coke?' 'So what do you think about that, huh, Randy?' He smiled and answered her, but I could see by the stiffness of his posture that this was hard for him.

'Well,' I said, 'tomorrow we turn around and head back. I have to say I'm ready.'

'I know what you mean,' Doris said. 'I'm getting tired of motels. I want to do some real traveling. Maybe that's my plan. Work at some job for a while and then go to Europe.'

'Oh, let's keep going,' Peg said happily. 'Let's go to California!'

'I think you've gone quite far enough,' Doris said sternly.

Peg looked as if she'd been hit. 'It's just that I've been having so much fun. I don't want it to end,' she said in a small voice.

Doris touched her hand. 'Hey, on the way back, we can go camp in the desert for a night, or do whatever you want. It'll be the best part of our vacation.' Doris said this brightly, although even she knew we wouldn't drive back in the way we had come, meandering along two-lane roads and stopping at every overlook and souvenir shop. No, we would take the highways, driving in shifts, and if we made Memphis in three days, it wouldn't be soon enough.

'Umm,' Randy said, his eyes darting around the table. 'I've been thinking. I have to get ready for college and everything, you know? So if you all want to take your time getting back, maybe I should take the bus.'

'Oh geez,' Peg wailed. 'Why is everyone against me? What did I do wrong?'

Randy put his arm around her. 'Look, never

155

mind—I didn't mean it. I'm just worried, you know, about getting back.'

Then Peg's freckled face squeezed into itself, as if she were gathering herself to cry. I thought she would cry later, when they lay together in their bed, and he would stroke her back and tell her he was sorry.

'It's just . . . it's that I have a lot to do,' Randy added. He tried to catch my eye, but I flinched away from his gaze. I knew this is how it would be from now on: Randy and me—Peg, too, in her own way—would be caught on the barbs of each others' words and glances, like fish caught on hooks and pulled along by invisible lines of hurt.

I decided it was best to change the subject. 'Are you looking forward to college, Randy?' I asked in a false voice.

And so we spoke no more of our plans.

THAT NIGHT, WE sat on Doris's hotel bed to watch the news. First the Democratic convention—bits of a speech by Humphrey, cheering delegates waving signs. And then the streets outside, the protestors falling back as the police swung their clubs like they were whacking at weeds. Young men and women dropping to their knees, covering their heads. The police standing in a circle, beating at whatever lay in the center. The empty street strewn with shoes and purses and scarves—all those pieces of themselves that people had left behind.

When Doris had first snapped on the TV, I'd settled on the bed to watch. Randy had sprawled on the floor in front of me, Peg beside him. At some point, Randy had shifted position, sitting up so he could lean against the bed, one hand hidden under the ruffled trim of the bedspread, inches away from my foot.

I was watching those blurry images on TV and suddenly I felt a touch on bare ankle. I bit my lip: he was stroking the ridge of my Achilles tendon and soft skin at the back of my heel. And all of it went on under the bedspread. If anyone had looked, they would have seen—what?—maybe a bulge in the fabric behind my foot, that was all.

I should have moved away from him. I wanted to—one part of me did, anyway. But I couldn't move. His fingers grazing my skin sent me into a trance of pleasure. I was greedy for that kind of pleasure. And suddenly I understood how weak the sensible part of me had become—nothing but a pip-squeak voice scolding in my head. Some other part of me had taken over now, a reckless Frannie, a greedy woman. So I let him continue. The touch of his fingers seemed run up my body and sing along my spine. I shivered; the skin on my arms gathered into goosepimples.

Through the half-slits of my eyes, I continued to watch the TV. A young man, his hands in an empty choke-hold, sprinted toward a policeman. The two of them locked for a moment in a sort of waltz, tottering like dancing bears, before they fell to the ground. That deadly slow dance on the TV screen and the delicious tickle of Randy's hand brushing my ankle—these went together, two pieces of evidence that my life would never be its sleepy self again.

'The world has just gone and changed on

157

us,' my father used to say. He said it when they sent that monkey up into space, and when stamps went from three cents to four, and when the first color TV sets started showing up in our town. He said it like he'd been betrayed, as if sometime in the thirties the world had promised him it wouldn't change, and here it was cheating on him again.

I remember my father in his starched shirt and bow tie sitting at the kitchen table with some papers spread before him. At night, it must have been. My mother stood at the sink, doing the dishes, and the two of them talked lazily. I had just come inside from a fall evening—kickball or jumprope with the neighbor children. My cheeks held the cold, tingling. As I bounded into the room, the two of them turned toward me, smiling, as if they'd been waiting for me all along.

158

Moments like that, we forgot about history. Then, we imagined no world existed outside our house, with its particular creaks and smell of steaming laundry. After dinner was when we had that feeling most of all, when we sat crammed around the card table playing a game. It seemed we'd always be the same—mother in her bibbed apron, smoking as she drew her cards; Dad half-listening for the phone to ring; Doris biting her tongue in concentration; me studying the pictures of kings and queens. We sat in those same chairs almost every night, four square. At those times, content and forgetful, we lived nowhere but in our New Hampshire town, a place that was as prim as an unsullied woman but nonetheless visited by the miracle of red-etched leaves falling in patterns of extraordinary significance.